A checklist of what Noelle wanted in a date for her sister's wedding:

❑ He had to look good in a suit.

❑ He had to be able to make social chitchat.

❑ Most importantly, he had to be completely forgettable so she could go back to her regular, work-filled, no-time-to-date dull life.

What she actually got:

✓ A devilishly handsome bad boy who preferred *un*dressing to dressing.

✓ Chitchat? The man was a certified flirt! She had to fight the other bridesmaids off him!

✓ Forgettable? Yeah—if she was suddenly struck with amnesia. She'd *never* forget one hot second for the rest of her completely changed life....

Dear Reader,

Picture this: you're a single woman and you still haven't met Mr. Right. You're not even fretting about this as you drive along the highway, when suddenly, *boom!* A fender bender. You're steaming mad—until you notice the other driver is tall, dark and *very* apologetic as he hands over his name and address in the form of his license and registration.

Of course I'm not suggesting you should try this at home. But it sure works for Maggie Donner in Lass Small's *Not Looking for a Texas Man.* (Especially once they're stuck together in his truck, waiting for help—*overnight.*)

An easier way to meet the man of your dreams is to buy him. And that's exactly what Noelle Perry does in Tiffany White's *Male for Sale.* Imagine: you're dateless for your *younger* sister's wedding, so you secretly buy a hunk at a bachelor auction—and hope he'll exchange his black leather jacket for a tuxedo. I know, money can't buy love—but maybe it can buy Noelle a date for the next three thousand Saturday nights.

Next month, look for two new entertaining, engaging Yours Truly novels by Cait London and Toni Collins— with two more unexpected ways to meet, date…and marry Mr. Right!

Yours truly,

Melissa Senate

Editor

Please address questions and book requests to:
Silhouette Reader Service
U.S.: 3010 Walden Ave., P.O. Box 1325, Buffalo, NY 14269
Canadian: P.O. Box 609, Fort Erie, Ont. L2A 5X3

TIFFANY WHITE

Male for Sale

SILHOUETTE YOURS TRULY™

Published by Silhouette Books
America's Publisher of Contemporary Romance

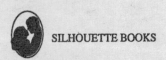 SILHOUETTE BOOKS

ISBN 0-373-52003-4

MALE FOR SALE

Copyright © 1995 by Anna Eberhardt

This edition published by arrangement with Harlequin Books S.A.

® and TM are trademarks of Harlequin Books S.A., used under license. Trademarks indicated with ® are registered in the United States Patent and Trademark Office, the Canadian Trade Marks Office and in other countries.

Printed in U.S.A.

About the author

When asked to describe her life, **TIFFANY WHITE** told us that in her fantasies she flies to the Coast for weekend visits with friends, sees all the latest movies, fills her closets with the latest fashions and regularly wins the *Romantic Times* Most Sensual Author Award.

In reality, Tiffany—a bestselling author for Harlequin Temptation—has gone to her office dressed in sweatshirts and leggings, has written four books in the past year, goes home to veg out with videos and has become the Susan Lucci of the coveted *Romantic Times* Award.

Prologue

➤◄

Noelle Perry was royally bummed out. She glared at the pristine white gold-lettered invitation to her baby sister Sophie's wedding. Frowning at the piece of parchment that had mocked her for the past five weeks, she cried out in exasperation, "Damn, Sophie—why did you have to go all traditional now? Why couldn't you have stayed true to character and eloped?"

Noelle had yet to come up with a man to attend Sophie's wedding as her escort. And there was *no way* she was going back home to St. Louis for the wedding without a male in tow. She wasn't up to enduring a barrage of grilling questions from relatives and smug looks from old boyfriends.

In frustration, she tossed the invitation onto a pile of papers on her desk. It landed on a bright blue sheet—an invitation to attend the "Male for Sale" bachelor auction at the Fairmont Hotel.

She picked up the blue paper, studied it, and made her decision.

1

Noelle stood outside the Moulin Rouge Room at the Fairmont Hotel, astonished that she'd actually gone through with her decision. Okay, she was pretty desperate and time was running out, but still... Half embarrassed she glanced around the corridor before picking up a "Male for Sale" catalogue from the stack on a table by the door.

She was certain she could afford the bidding. One of the reasons she'd relocated to Chicago from St. Louis was the higher salary she'd been offered.

Her only consolation for what she was about to do tonight was the fact that the money would go to charity. Soothed by that justification, she carefully read through the paragraph describing each of the bachelors up for auction. Each bachelor was to spend a weekend with the woman who bid the highest for him.

In Noelle's case, the lucky man would be spending the weekend as her date for Sophie's wedding. She could imagine just how *thrilled* the bachelor would be when he learned that little bit of news.

Unfortunately, there were no pictures to go with the bachelor profiles. Tonight's auction was unique in that the women were to bid on the bachelors "sight unseen" while the unidentified bachelors sat onstage. None of the women would learn the identity of the bachelor she'd bought until *after* she'd made her purchase.

Taking a deep breath, Noelle went inside the packed room and found a seat at one of the banquet tables. She looked around her and estimated that there were about two hundred chattering, excited women seated in the Moulin Rouge Room. Noelle sized up the crowd. There were a few women dressed as she was—in a business suit. But the majority were all glammed up as if they were trying to make an impression.

At least, in keeping with the discreet nature of the auction, no press or television cameras were allowed. Noelle's only fear was that one of the bachelors would turn out to be a member of the banking community. As a bank vice president, she'd be mortified if she ended up purchasing some banking professional who would spread the news that she was so hard up that she had to buy a date for her sister's wedding.

That thought alone kept her from swallowing any of the delicious desserts on the table.

She smiled nervously at the women around her as the bachelors paraded out to take their seats onstage. If there was a banker among them, she didn't recognize him—thank God!

Hunter Ashton sat onstage wondering what sort of descriptive paragraph his sister had written up for him. He looked out over the sea of women and a grin took up residence on his lips. Come on, ladies, step right up, his grin said, I aim to enjoy.

Noelle looked at each of the bachelors in turn, trying to guess which was the one who went with the description that had caught her fancy. She was pretty sure it was the man in the gray double-breasted suit. He definitely would make a nice showing at the wedding.

At least she was sure it wasn't the bachelor at the end of the row. He certainly wasn't her idea of an escort for a formal wedding. The woman who bought him would be the type whose idea of paradise was a wild ride on a motorcycle.

The guy didn't even have the manners to sit up straight. Instead he leaned back with his legs sprawled apart. His tousled blond locks needed a trim. He'd left his long, slim-fitting navy jacket unbuttoned. Beneath it he wore a slate-gray polo shirt paler than the jacket. His body was lanky and lean and she would have had to be dead not to notice it. He had a certain arrogance—or was it mischievousness?—that would never do.

As the female emcee stepped up to the microphone to begin the auction, Noelle scanned the catalog to see if she could guess which profile belonged to that born-to-raise-hell bachelor. Physical characteristics such as height, weight, hair and eye color couldn't be mentioned, but she thought she had his description pegged anyway.

A good-looking stud. Adventurous and sensual. Interests include car races, windsurfing and riding my motorcycle.

The auction began. The first bachelor to be auctioned off was a jock.

The next bachelor up was the one whom she'd decided to bid on.

Attractive, college-educated professional. Generous, romantic twenty-eight-year-old with a variety of interests, including music, art and reading.

With her eyes glued to the bachelor in the gray double-breasted suit, she placed the opening bid. The bidding was spirited. A woman at the table next to hers stayed with the bidding all the way to seven hundred dollars. Determined and frustrated, Noelle finally called out, "One thousand dollars."

The other woman dropped out.

Noelle had paid more than she'd planned to, but she'd placed the highest bid and won her bachelor. Her worries were over.

But the guy in the gray business suit didn't stand.

None of the bachelors did until the female emcee with the long blond hair went over to the man at the end of the row and whispered something to him.

He stood then, to acknowledge he was the bachelor she'd bought with her bid of one thousand dollars.

Noelle tried not to faint.

She'd really gone and done it this time.

No way would her parents forget this guy by her next visit. She was bringing one more child home to play.

She'd grown up the only adult in her family. Her own parents shared a joy for life that was beyond Noelle's understanding. They went in and out of businesses on a whim. As a result their fortunes were a roller coaster of ups and downs. They'd moved from mansions to shacks.

No one in her family was responsible.

Except her.

And look what she'd bought to escort her to the wedding.

Peter Pan lived!

Maybe she could sneak out quietly and no one would notice. Going to the wedding alone would be preferable to showing up with the gorgeous outlaw who was now—oh, no!—heading toward her.

It was too late to run.

Too late to hide.

But not too late to faint.

Which she did, with none of the aplomb of a Southern belle. It wasn't a swoon. It was more like a slump.

"Stand back, everyone. Give the girl some air," came a masculine command as Noelle's eyes fluttered open and she heard the excited murmuring swirling around.

"Poor little thing just fainted from all the excitement of winning me," the same voice continued, cocky as hell.

"Hunter, will you shut up and let me take care of—"

"Oh, Daphne, chill out. I just saw her pretty brown eyes open. There's no blood, so she doesn't need a nurse. I'll just lift her up in my arms and take her outside for some air.''

"No!" Noelle couldn't understand why no one heeded her loud objection. She had screamed it, hadn't she? She moved her lips but no sound came out. She was helpless as the strong arms lifted her easily.

"All right, Hunter—but behave. I've got to finish up this auction. I'm counting on you to be a gentleman and take proper care of—''

"Noelle. Her name is Noelle," Hunter said. "Pretty name for a pretty lady. I thought so when she started bidding on me. I was hoping she could afford me. She's exactly my type: prim, proper and unapproachable with her dark hair pulled back in a tight knot, her blouse buttoned up to her throat. You know how I like a challenge. But truly I thought it would take more than five minutes to make her swoon."

"Don't be getting a swelled head, Hunter. Just take care of Noelle. I'll get back to you when I finish here."

"Yes, Daphne dear."

Noelle was wide-awake, but kept her eyes closed until Hunter began carrying her to the door.

"Would you please put me down, you . . . you . . ." she sputtered, unable to form a coherent word.

"Hunter. My name is Hunter," he said, whipping out that lethal grin of his.

"Okay, Hunter. Would you kindly put me down? I'm perfectly fine now."

"Oh, you won't get any argument from me on that score. You are a perfectly fine-looking woman."

But he still didn't put her down.

"I'll scream—"

"Now why would you want to do that?" he asked, genuinely puzzled.

"Because this was all a mistake. If you'll just put me down, I'll pay my bid and be gone. There is no need for you to honor your agreement for a weekend date. I'll consider the thousand dollars a charity donation for a good cause and be done with it."

"I don't understand," he said, putting her down. "Why did you bid on a date if you didn't want one? Weren't you planning on—"

"It was for a wedding, okay?" Noelle replied, figuring it would dissuade him. No man ever went willingly to a wedding—even the groom.

"A wedding! I love weddings."

"You do?" she responded, caught off guard by his exclamation of delight.

"Of course."

She didn't believe him—not for a minute. "You really love weddings?" she repeated.

"Are you kidding? All that virginal white, flowing champagne, and lust in the air. The only thing more explosive and exciting is the Fourth of July."

Noelle groaned. He was her worst nightmare. And she had the sinking feeling he was a nightmare that was going to be hard to banish. He was as persistent as a frisky puppy.

"It would be for the whole weekend with my family at their house," she began, in her effort to persuade him that escorting her to the wedding wasn't something he'd want to do. "You'd have to go to the rehearsal dinner. You'd have to attend the wedding and the reception. And any other family obligations involved—"

"Hell, I'll even go to the bachelor party," Hunter offered, way too agreeably.

"You would."

"What?" he asked, bending down to catch what she'd muttered under her breath.

"Nothing." She frowned. How on earth was she going to discourage him? She couldn't believe she was in the position of wanting to do so. All along she'd been working on arguments to get her bachelor to agree to escort her to Sophie's wedding. What a revolting development. It wasn't as if she'd had a lot of experience beating men off with a stick. Her mother and sister were the femmes fatales in the family. Somehow she hadn't inherited the flirting gene. It was probably for the best. No telling what sorts of trouble she'd have gotten herself into if she had. She might have married a wild man like her father or married at the tender age of eighteen—as Sophie was just about to do.

When *she* married, it would be a marriage of reason between two sensible adults.

"So..." Hunter prompted.

"I'm sorry?" Noelle said, not catching the drift of what he was asking.

"Are you going to keep me or return me and embarrass me before all the curious women inside?"

She hadn't thought of *that*. It wasn't in her nature to hurt anyone's feelings. Though she was fairly certain Hunter's pout was more for effect than real. She'd bet it would be next to impossible to embarrass Hunter.

"If you keep me, you can just give me the check and I'll turn it in for you so you don't have to go back inside, if you feel funny about having fainted in front of everyone," he offered, nudging her to make the decision in his favor.

Heavens, she'd never seen a man so anxious to get dressed up in a monkey suit. Maybe he cleaned up real nice. Maybe he'd behave. Maybe it wouldn't be such a bad idea.

Maybe she was crazy.

But she wrote out a check and gave it to him anyway.

"Aren't you forgetting something?" he asked, pocketing the check she'd made out to the hospital for a thousand smackers.

"A thousand dollars, right? That was the sum I bid—"

"Yes, that's right. I'm talking about your address. If I'm going to escort you to this shindig, I'm going to have to know where to pick you up."

She gave him her address, which wasn't on her check. She used a post-office box number on her checks. A single woman couldn't be too careful. You never knew what kind of loony would take a liking to you.

One like Hunter.

Unfortunately, it was too late to reconsider and give him a fake address. Besides, for some strange reason, Hunter was determined to go to the wedding with her.

"You're smiling," Hunter observed. "You should do that more often. You're really pretty when you smile."

"I already said you could go," Noelle returned, not about to be taken in by a smooth talker.

"So you did. Just tell me where and what time you want me to bring the carriage 'round to pick you up and we'll call it a night. We don't want you getting faint on me again."

"I need to leave for St. Louis—did I mention the wedding is in St. Louis? Maybe you won't want to go out of town on such short notice. Your boss might object," she said, still snatching at straws to wiggle out of the deal.

"My boss won't object," he assured her.

"I'll want to get an early start—say, seven—so I'll have time to freshen up for the rehearsal dinner after the six-hour drive."

"No problem," he continued to assure her.

She played what she believed was her trump card with a flourish: "I need to leave this Thursday morning. The wedding is *this* weekend."

"Perfect."

"Perfect?"

"Right. I just finished a long project and my boss wants me to take some time off to recharge my batteries, so to speak."

"Your boss is . . ."

"Me," he supplied with a wicked wink.

"Tell me, Valerie, love . . . if you could date any superhero, whom would you date?" Hunter Ashton asked, looking at the disaster area his home office had become. He knew he ought to clean it, but he was too tired. The end of a project always left him feeling completely drained of energy. But he was never too tired for the mental conversations he held with the blond amazon cartoon character he'd created. With her swing of long blond hair, buxom curves, legs that went on forever and savvy attitude, Valerie seemed real to him.

"A superhero?" Valerie repeated, considering her options.

"Right." Hunter made a halfhearted attempt to pick up some of the clutter. "I know. I bet you'd choose Superman, wouldn't you? After all, he is the primo superhero."

"No, it wouldn't be Superman."

"Really?" Easily distracted, Hunter gave up on tidying and sprawled his length over the sofa to consider. "Why not?"

Valerie came over to the sofa and perched on the armrest. Swinging her long legs, she turned toward Hunter and gave him a disdainful look. "Are you kidding? What woman would want to date a man who's faster than a speeding bullet?"

"*Valerie!*"

"Well, you asked," she said, flicking back the mane of long, thick blond hair.

"Okay, then how about Spiderman? Do you think women like men with big feet?" he asked, straying from the subject as he kicked off his sneakers and stared at his own size twelves.

"Spiderman never blinks...too creepy. As for big feet— You know what they say about men with big feet...."

Hunter smiled, waving his toes. "Batman," he suggested.

"Pu-lease. He hangs out with Robin *all* the time. Three would be a crowd."

Hunter stretched and yawned. "Spawn, then. He's a moody, romantic superhero."

"Angst, but no angst. He's hung up forever on his first love."

Hunter shrugged in agreement and reached for the comics section of the newspaper scattered beneath the coffee table.

"How about the Green Hornet?"

"I'm not into insects."

"Plastic Man..."

"Too artificial."

"Wait a minute." Hunter snapped his fingers and sat up. "I'm forgetting about the perfect alpha male superhero— Wolverine."

"No way. I don't want claw marks on my back." She stretched and arched her back. "Besides, haven't you seen the cover of *Mouth to Mouth?* Wolverine is into supermodel Claudia Schiffer."

"Who isn't?" Hunter said, picturing the supermodel in a sexy outfit, something racy red. After a brief erotic detour of the mind he returned to the subject at hand. "Okay, I'm out of guesses. You tell me."

Valerie snapped her fingers. "Captain Marvel, of course."

"Captain Marvel? Why would you choose Captain Marvel?"

"Because, silly, I'd want to find out what's so bloody marvelous about him."

"You're such a princess."

"You know, Hunter Ashton, you ought to get out more. See other women."

"But I like you, princess. You're so lush and full of life. You're always ready for adventure."

"You don't think maybe I'm a little too lush . . . ?" she asked. Glancing down at her ample cleavage, she tugged her bustier up.

"Hey, lush works for Wolverine," he reminded her. "Besides, I like women who are bigger than life. You know. Big hair, big . . . ah . . . and a big cape."

"You're such a pervert, Hunter. Don't you think it's a little odd for a grown man like you to want to dress me up in thigh-high boots and skimpy outfits?"

"No. I think you look way cool."

"So why didn't you name me the Ice Princess?"

"Because Valerie Valor, the Viking Princess of Venus, is a proper name for a superheroine. Aren't you being a bit ungrateful? After all, I've turned you into the bestselling comic-book character you are."

"Maybe I'm tired of being good all the time."

"Don't tell me you want to be a bad girl—"

"What's wrong with that?"

"It involves a lot of erasing."

"Not the eraser! Please, Hunter, don't rub me out. I'll be good. I promise."

"I know."

* * *

"You need a keeper," Daphne Ashton chided her twin brother, Hunter. "This whole apartment looks like a frat house—after a keg party." She lifted a pair of socks gingerly and dropped them into the wicker basket with the rest of the clothing she'd collected.

Hunter looked up from the splash page he'd just added one final touch to, reluctant to let go of his latest project. Stretching his lanky frame, he rolled his neck from side to side, as it was still stiff from the long hours spent drawing. "I was on deadline, sister dear. You know I can't be creative and domestic at the same time. I'll clean now that I've finished Valerie Valor's latest adventure." He fiddled with his white leather-thong bracelet while Daphne sliced him a considering look that said they both knew there wasn't *any* time when Hunter wasn't being "creative."

"Why are you here, Daphne? We both know you didn't come over to clean my apartment."

"Can't a sister visit her brother—"

"She can, but you hardly ever do. You're always busy in the emergency room at Cook County."

"Northwestern," Daphne corrected.

"Whatever. Don't you have some patients at the hospital to torture? Or is it a slow day in the windy city? What, no political candidates shooting themselves in the foot today...?"

"It's my day off. You have heard of a day off? You should try giving the concept a try, you know. Never can tell, you might even like it. At least it would give you some perspective on the fantasy world you live in most of the time. I worry about you sometimes, Hunter.''

"Yeah, you *and* Valerie."

She arched an eyebrow. Startling blue eyes the same color as his censured him. "See what I mean?"

"Why are you here, Daphne?" Hunter asked again, refusing to bite on an old ongoing dialogue between them.

Daphne set the basket down. "Okay, you're right. I came over here to ask you a big favor."

"Sure, whatever you need," Hunter agreed, reaching for a cloth to wipe off his pen point.

"But you haven't even heard what the favor is."

"Does it matter? You know you'll only wheedle it out of me whatever it is, anyway, Daphne."

"But aren't you even a little bit curious?"

Hunter put down the cloth he was using and began paying attention. "You know the rules. As long as it doesn't involve any hospital-type stuff. You know how I am around blood."

Daphne slid down onto the sofa. "I can't believe you faint at the sight of blood and I'm a trauma nurse. Are you sure you weren't adopted?"

"We're twins," Hunter said, deliberately rubbing it in.

"If you're such a wuss, Hunter, how come you have Valerie Valor pummeling everyone in the comic series?"

"Hey, women love Valerie doing in the bad guys. That's a big part of why my series is such a success. Valerie is my strike at equality for women. My comic is more than just entertainment—Valerie is a role model for women.''

Daphne choked out a laugh. ''Yeah, in the comics. A status quo, long-legged, big-busted blonde who performs her job wearing a red bustier,'' she said, throwing her hands up in exasperation.

''Oh, like guys don't get off on seeing you coming with your blond hair, blue eyes and nurse whites. They probably think they're already dead and gone to heaven.''

Daphne just shook her head and closed her eyes. When she opened them, her gaze fell on a catalog on the edge of the table beside his drawing board. She recognized the cover. ''Dare I ask why you're reading a Victoria's Secret catalog, Hunter?''

Hunter shrugged. ''I was thinking about updating Valerie's wardrobe.''

''You've got to get out more, Hunter.''

''I am. This weekend, as a matter of fact. I'm going to a wedding.''

''Wedding?''

''The babe who bought me wants to take me.''

''Which brings me to the favor. I want you to behave on this date, okay? I organized the bachelor auction benefit. It was my idea. I don't want the whole thing to blow up in my face because you...''

''Aw, come on, Daphne....''

''Just behave.''

''I'll make them love me, I promise.''

''See that you do.''

''Whatcha doing?''

Noelle looked over her shoulder at Barbara Ann, the chubby, brown-haired seven-year-old who lived across the hall in the apartment building. Barbara Ann's mother was a single parent and occasionally worked overtime. It was understood that Barbara Ann would wait in Noelle's apartment until her mother arrived home.

"Painting my toenails for the wedding."

"Oh. Did you find a dress? You said it had to be perfect."

"Yes, I found one," Noelle said, finished painting her toenails. She put the stopper back in the bottle. "Want to see it?"

"Can I?" Barbara Ann's dark brown eyes were saucer wide.

"Sure, come on, it's in my closet. You can see my shoes I had dyed to match, too." Noelle led the way to her peach bedroom. Like the rest of the apartment, the decor was soft and pretty, but not homey.

Barbara Ann crawled up on the floral-print bedspread and sat cross-legged with her chin cupped in her hands, waiting.

Noelle withdrew her dress for the wedding from the closet. It was the one thing about Sophie's wedding that had gone right for her so far. The dress was perfect.

Pale celery green, it had a high jewel neckline and long sleeves. From the wrist to about two inches from the elbow, a row of tiny silk-covered buttons decorated each sleeve.

"Well . . . what do you think?" Noelle asked.

"It's not very fancy, is it?"

"You don't like it?" Noelle asked, surprised.

"Well, I thought it might be red," Barbara Ann said, raising and lowering her shoulders.

"Red?"

"It's my favorite color," Barbara Ann announced. "Are your shoes red?"

"No, they match the dress."

"Oh."

Noelle picked up a pair of white dress gloves and held them up for Barbara Ann's approval. "Do you like my gloves?"

"They're all right." Tilting her head, the seven-year-old thought a moment, then asked, "Are you going to wear a hat to the wedding? Do you have a hat?"

"No, no hat."

"When I was a flower girl, I wore a ring of flowers in my hair. You could do that," she suggested. "They smelled real nice, and they had ribbon streamers."

"A garland."

"What?"

"The flowers you wore in your hair are called a garland. I bet you were a very pretty flower girl."

"I got sick."

"You did?"

"Uh-huh. I ate too much wedding cake and ice cream."

"Would you like some ice cream now?" Noelle asked, searching for something Barbara Ann might like.

She hated that the child she adored might find her boring. If only she could abandon herself enough to play.

She had a feeling her bachelor-auction date for Sophie's wedding was going to be just as bored with her dress as Barbara Ann was.

And worse, that she was going to be the most boring date of Hunter Ashton's life.

Noelle's week went smoothly until Wednesday, despite her constant misgivings about her escort for Sophie's wedding.

On Wednesday, however, things began to go awry.

First, the corporate account she'd been working to acquire requested a male vice-president. The patriarch of the wine company didn't cotton to a woman handling his money. There wasn't much she could do, because you could hardly sue the customer.

To counter the slant against women in banking, in all the public speaking she did, she encouraged women to get over their fear of math and money, and take charge of their finances.

She then returned to worrying about what could go wrong with the wedding, starting with the word *carriage,* which Hunter had used when he'd said he would pick her up.

A carriage could be anything from a low rider to a motorcycle.

Please, not the motorcycle, she prayed daily.

And again Thursday morning as she stood waiting for Hunter to arrive.

Her palms were sweaty and her imagination was racing when the doorbell rang.

But it wasn't Hunter who greeted her. Instead it was Barbara Ann.

"What are you doing home this time of the morning?" Noelle asked.

"I'm home from school 'cause I didn't feel so good this morning."

"Where's your mom?"

"She stayed home with me. She's on the computer with her office. She said I could come over and say hi to you before you left for work, but I wasn't to bother you. Am I bothering you?"

"No, of course not. Come on in. I'm waiting for my— Actually, I'm waiting for Prince Charming to arrive to take me to the wedding."

"But you're not dressed up in your pretty dress."

"I'm taking it with me. The wedding isn't until Saturday night. Tonight is the rehearsal dinner and casual, sort of."

"Oh."

"So, what's wrong with you, Barbara Ann? You got a tummyache or a spelling test?"

"I just feel yucky...."

"Yeah, I know the feeling," Noelle said, having had a rather unsettled stomach herself that morning.

"Do you want something to eat?" Noelle offered.

Barbara Ann shook her head no.

"Not even a Popsicle? I have cherry. It's your favorite color...."

"Okay. But don't tell Mom. I didn't eat any breakfast."

Noelle knew she wouldn't have to tell "Mom"—the red-stained lips would give their secret away. But she figured it was okay to indulge Barbara Ann since she wasn't feeling well.

Barbara Ann was halfway through her Popsicle and only just started on her questions about Prince Charming when a honking racket started up outside the apartment building.

Did motorcycles have horns? Noelle wondered.

She didn't want to look, so she sent Barbara Ann to the window.

"Wow!" Barbara Ann pronounced. "It's a really big long car."

"Is it black?" Noelle ventured, visualizing a hearse as a worst-case scenario.

"Nope. It's white."

"White!"

"Uh-huh...and some guy's waving at the apartment building while he's standing beside the big car honking the horn. I think he wants you to come down."

Noelle took a deep breath and closed her eyes. "Is he wearing a suit?" she asked hopefully.

"Uh-uh. He's got on jeans and a baseball cap. The cap's on his head the wrong way."

Backward—of course. Noelle opened her eyes. "He does have a shirt on, doesn't he?" she inquired, picking up her suitcase and purse before he woke everyone in the building, including the retired mailman.

"Uh-huh. It's pink."

"Pink?"

"Uh-huh. Pink. He's tall."

"I know."

"Is he a good kisser?"

"Barbara Ann!"

"Well, my cousin says—"

"Don't you listen to what your cousin says. You're entirely too young to know about kissing."

"Oh." Barbara Ann didn't sound all that convinced.

The racket continued as Noelle shooed Barbara Ann out into the hall with her bare Popsicle stick.

"I can't take this, Mom'll know," Barbara Ann said, handing Noelle the stick. "Will you tell me all about the wedding when you come back?"

"Yes," Noelle agreed, locking the apartment door.

"And show me the bride's bouquet, if you catch it?"

"I'm *not* catching it."

"But you might," Barbara Ann insisted.

Not if she could dodge it, Noelle vowed to herself.

"Bye!" Barbara Ann waved as Noelle went down the stairs.

She was going to kill Hunter when she was done with him. A slow . . . painful . . . embarrassing—

"Good morning," Hunter said brightly, holding open the trunk of the limo.

"Is this what you do? Are you a limo driver?" Noelle asked, as he placed her suitcase and the wedding gift in the trunk.

"Not right now. I used to, though. That's how I got the limo for the wedding. It wasn't rented for the weekend."

Used to. That probably meant Hunter was unemployed and explained why he was so anxious to take her to the wedding. It meant plenty of free meals.

And flowing champagne.

She groaned inwardly as he closed the trunk and went around to open the door for her. All she wanted was for the weekend to be over so she could get back to her nice, safe, sane life.

"Do you always eat Popsicles for breakfast?" Hunter asked, nodding at the stick in her hand as they pulled away.

"No, it's— Oh, never mind."

"Cherry, huh? My favorite flavor..."

She glared over at him.

"Red's my favorite color," he explained.

"Here, have it. It's all yours," she said, shoving the Popsicle at him. "Enjoy."

A seven-year-old. She was going home to her sister's wedding with a man who shared a seven-year-old's taste for cherry Popsicles.

It couldn't get any worse.

Barbara Ann sat in the window seat at her bedroom window and spied on Noelle and her Prince Charming. She thought she'd look a lot happier if she were Noelle. She began to imagine herself older and in a pretty red dress. To imagine she was the one being picked up to go to a fancy ball in a long white limo.

She was so caught up in her fantasy, she didn't even notice the limo pull away or hear her mother come into her bedroom.

"Where have you been, Barbara Ann? You didn't go bother Noelle, did you?" Barbara Ann's mother asked upon seeing her daughter's red lips.

"I only went to say goodbye. Did you see the guy who came to take her to the wedding? Cousin Missy would call him a hunk. I bet he's a good kisser. Missy says—"

"Barbara Ann!"

"Aw, Mom, I know about kissing," Barbara Ann said, a worldly seven.

"Barbara Ann, you're *contagious.*"

"Constageous? What's that?"

"The doctor just called and confirmed you have the chicken pox."

That afternoon the sun came out from behind the clouds to play hide-and-seek in Noelle's empty apartment. The splash of light traveled across the plush peach carpet, up over the floral-print bedspread and over to the open closet where it reflected off the clear plastic bag covering the celery-green dress hanging forlornly on the door.

The late-afternoon sun caught the bugle beads on the cap sleeves of Sophie's wedding gown, shooting off sparkly prisms of light as she turned to model it for her mother.

"What do you think?" Sophie asked, uncharacteristically shy and unsure. Sophie and her mother not only resembled each other physically, both were of the same temperament. Headstrong and spoiled, Sophie was having prewedding jitters.

Grace got up from the beige brocade chair in the ornate dressing room of the bridal shop. She hugged her daughter's shoulders from behind. "I think that if you get stood up at the altar, there will be lots of volunteers to take the groom's place. Besides what man would have the nerve to stand up a redhead? We're not well known for our tempers for nothing.''

"Oh, Mother you don't think that—"

Grace, more petite than her daughter, pulled Sophie around to face her. "No, of course not, darling. You're going to be a beautiful bride. The wedding will be perfect. Trust me."

"It will, won't it?" Sophie said, her dark eyes brightening. "And you know what? I've got it all worked out with everyone so that Noelle catches the bridal bouquet!"

"I'm afraid, dear, that it's going to take more than a bridal bouquet to get your older sister to the altar," Grace said, with a weary sigh.

Sophie grinned, lifting a padded hanger from a hook on the wall and smiling at her mother. "You mean something like what Daddy did to get you to marry him."

"How did you— Oh, you mean the kidnapping. Yes, a kidnapping might do the trick. Only I was a willing hostage. Something tells me Noelle would go kicking and screaming."

Sophie began removing her wedding gown. "She is coming to the wedding, isn't she? Every time I've talked to her in the past six weeks, she sounded vague."

"She's coming. She called this morning."

"Is she bringing a date?"

"Well, to tell the truth, she did sound a little vague about that when I asked."

2

$\longrightarrow \leftarrow$

They settled into an uncomfortable silence on the drive out of Chicago. Since he had the urge to talk to *someone,* he began a mental conversation with Valerie.

"Well, Valerie, now what am I going to do? Noelle won't even talk to me."

"So you talk to her. You're the one who always puts words in my mouth."

"But this time I don't know what to say. You gotta help me out, here."

"Are you gonna get me out of this red bustier and into something decent?" Valerie reminded.

"Look, Superwoman doesn't complain about her outfit. Why can't you be more like her?"

"Because I'm a woman of the nineties. That's how you created me. You know. With a mind of my own."

"That was a mistake."

"What did you say?" Valerie demanded.

"I said, what kind of outfit did you have in mind? Not that I'm agreeing to anything, you understand."

"I'd settle for a sports bra and biker shorts," Valerie suggested. "At least I'd be comfortable."

"I'll think about it."

"And remember I like pink."

"Pink!"

"Pink."

"But you can't pummel people in pink."

"So make me more charming. I'll use my brain and my wiles instead of my fists."

"We'll talk about it later. Right now I've got to figure out what I'm going to say to Noelle."

"Talk to her about the wedding."

"You think?"

"Well, you've got to find out what your role is. Are you supposed to be a first date, a boyfriend, a lover, or a fiancé?"

"Good question."

"So ask it, dufus...."

Hunter cleared his throat and banished Valerie Valor from his mind as he decided how to phrase the question she had brought up. It would certainly break the ice.

"Uh, I was wondering."

Noelle turned to him.

"You've changed your mind," she said on a note of wistful hope.

"No, of course not." Why was she so anxious to be rid of him? Here he was, all primed for an adventure, and he'd hooked up with someone who seemed determined to avoid it and him at all costs. "Maybe you could explain something to me," he said, glancing over at her. "I'm curious to know why you bought me for this wedding, when apparently you don't want to go with me."

She didn't deny it. He watched her smooth her hand over the plush seat of the limo while she chose her words of reply.

"I didn't exactly mean to buy you," she said finally. There was so much room between them in the huge car that her voice almost echoed.

"I don't understand." Hunter eased the limo up to a stoplight just before the entry ramp onto the interstate.

"Well," she began a little hesitantly, twirling a strand of her long dark chestnut-colored hair. "Uh, as you may recall, the women bidding on the bachelors didn't know which bachelor in particular we were bidding on until we'd bought him."

"Oh, so you're saying that you're— You're saying that you're disappointed with the...with me."

"I wouldn't put it that way."

"Well, how would you put it, then?" The light changed and he headed through the intersection, having to slam on his brakes when someone ran a red light at the last second.

Hunter threw his arm out to brace Noelle from flying against the dash. Because of the distance between them, only his hand broke her slide.

"Are you okay?"

"Yeah, I'm okay. I don't believe the idiots who take such chances."

"Chances with other people's lives..."

Noelle nodded.

He eased the limo through the intersection and onto the entry ramp while she resettled herself on the seat.

"Who did you think you were bidding on when you bought me?" he asked, once he'd melded into the high-speed traffic on the inside lane.

"The guy in the gray business suit."

"You're kidding. He looked pretty boring to me."

"I was looking for boring."

"I could be boring."

Noelle shot a glance over at him. "Not even on a good day."

"What's wrong with having fun? It's a wedding, after all."

"Maybe you're right. Maybe I should throw caution to the wind and treat this as a weekend 'adventure'. No. This whole thing has been an ill-conceived idea. It'll teach me to never do something on impulse again."

"Don't you want to go to your sister's wedding?"

"Of course I do."

"You just didn't want to show up alone, right? Why? Because you're older than she is?"

Noelle shook her head no. "You're a guy. You'd never understand."

"Sure I would. My twin sister, Daphne—you met her, she was running the bachelor auction—she says I can read her mind."

"Can you read mine?"

"No, but then I don't know you that well. Maybe if we talked I could get to know you better and help you out here. You might as well enjoy the wedding since you're going."

Noelle stared out the limo window and then looked away. Another car passing them on the highway had gawking passengers trying to discern if someone famous was in the limo.

"Why did you have to bring this limo? Everyone will be looking at us."

"It was an ill-conceived idea. It'll teach me to never do something on impulse again," he offered, repeating her phrase.

It got a smile.

"So, are we lovers?"

That got a frown.

"I mean, what exactly are you planning to tell people about me? I have to know to play my part."

"Oh, no, you're an unemployed actor, aren't you? This is going to be a disaster, I just know it."

"Calm down. I'm not an unemployed actor. I'm only trying to help, here. Don't you agree we have to get our stories straight? Or do you really want me to tell everyone that you bought a date to bring you to the wedding?"

"No!"

"My point exactly. Not that I think there's anything wrong with it. It's a great adventure. That's why I insisted on Daphne letting me be in the auction."

"A great adventure," Noelle repeated on a groan. "You think this is going to be a great adventure—"

"You know what I mean. We can make this work."

"We can?"

"Sure. Just tell me how I can help."

Noelle was silent for a moment, considering.

"Okay. I came to the bachelor auction because I've been so busy with my career, I haven't had time for dating. I didn't want to go home for the wedding and face a lot of questions from relatives about why I wasn't married and having babies. I thought if I at least showed up with a man, they'd be inclined to think I was involved.''

"Your career. I should know what it is that you do.''

"I'm vice president of a bank. Chicago Fidelity Trust.''

Hunter whistled, impressed. "I'd say you were a real handy person to know.''

"I turn down more loans than I approve,'' she was quick to point out. That had been a great move, telling an unemployed person she was a bank vice-president.

"I'll bet you do.''

Hunter marveled at the way she went from being a bit shy and insecure to being very in control and sure about her career. One thing was for certain, she was the prettiest bank vice president he'd ever met—and he'd met a lot of them when he'd been trying to finance his own comic book.

Her porcelain skin glowed and made him want to touch her. Her full pink lips were bait she didn't even know she had. Kissing them crossed his mind a lot. He was afraid behaving like a gentleman wasn't going to be easy.

"So, what kind of relationship did you have in mind?''

"What?''

"For the relatives.''

"Something just short of a fiancé. I don't want them throwing me a shower, for heaven's sake. We've been dating a while and we're ... friends.''

"*Good* friends?"

"Okay, good friends. But I don't want you getting any ideas. This is only for the relatives' benefit. When it's over, it's over."

"But you might change your mind. I can be very charming."

"I'm sure. But I'm very busy. I don't have—"

"Time for romance. I know."

They drifted into silence again as the rolling green hills of the countryside flashed past.

Hunter reached to turn on the stereo for some Kenny G.

Within moments Noelle had drifted off to sleep, he saw when he glanced over as they passed the halfway mark on the drive to St. Louis.

Valerie was lounging on the hood of the limo, her long blond hair blowing in the breeze. "Now what, Valerie? My conversation was so stimulating I put her to sleep."

"Let her sleep," Valerie said, unconcerned. "She's tired. Probably had a rough week. She'll come around."

"But she said she's too busy for romance."

Valerie stood on the hood of the limo pretending to be a hood ornament; she really needed a sailing ship to do her justice. "No woman is too busy for romance. You've got to show her what she's missing. Turn on the old Hunter Ashton charm. Sweep Ms. Noelle Perry off her feet."

"But Daphne told me to behave."

"Daphne," Valerie snorted. "Daphne is just like Noelle. They both could do with a little more fun in their lives."

"Fun, huh? Okay, I'll see what I can do to put some fun in this weekend. Though I suspect I'm going to have to drag Ms. Perry kicking and screaming into it. Her smile is about as rusty as the gate hinge of a neglected garden."

"Then buy her something pink. That'll cheer her up."

"No. Red. Red's better."

Valerie sighed, resigned. She lay back down on the hood, draping herself provocatively. "Just as long as it isn't a bustier."

"Why not?"

Valerie smiled seductively. "Because only I can carry off a red bustier."

Hunter left Valerie to her ego while he thought about ways to make Noelle enjoy the wedding weekend. He liked to make people feel good—it made him feel good to make others feel good. He liked everyone to have a good time; it was just that lately he'd begun to notice that *he* wasn't. Transient good times weren't as satisfying as they once had been.

Even Valerie was getting cranky.

Noelle wasn't asleep any longer.

She'd woken up when Hunter had stopped for gas, a quart of milk and a handful of Twinkies. Still, she pretended to be asleep as they passed through the tall cornfields near the border of Missouri. In half an hour they'd be at her parents' house. She needed the time to collect her thoughts.

A wedding was sure to be fraught with chaos in her family, especially since—at the moment—her parents were in the money. If they hadn't been, they probably would have bought Sophie a ladder to elope.

If only Noelle could have begged off the wedding, claiming she was ill. At the moment her stomach could lay legitimate claim to queasiness.

But the excuse wouldn't work anyway, with her loony family. They'd probably just bring the wedding to her.

Her loony family...

Why did she have to be the only sane one of them?

If she ever decided to get married, she'd have to do it before the prospective groom met her family. She wondered how Sophie had managed to hold on to her fiancé after he'd met the family. It didn't bode well for Marky that he hadn't bolted, to date.

It could mean one of two things.

She was either getting a brother-in-law who was a saint, or, after their marriage, Noelle would still be the only sane one in the family.

With a name like Marky, she didn't hold out much hope for sainthood.

Not for the first time, she wondered if perhaps she hadn't been adopted. When she'd voiced that particular concern out loud, the whole family had laughed—said she was being silly.

Silly indeed.

She'd never been silly a day in her life.

Her thoughts drifted back to the impending wedding. It wasn't that she didn't wish her baby sister well. She did. Though, at eighteen, she wasn't sure Sophie knew enough about love—knew enough about anything—to make such a lifetime commitment.

Maybe she was just jealous. At twenty-eight, Noelle had begun to notice how much of the world was divided up into couples. It would be convenient to have a permanent escort, but to marry a man for convenience wasn't her speed.

For all her practicality, Noelle was a romantic at heart. But she didn't want just some smooth talker. She wanted a man of substance.

The right man for her would have to sweep her off her feet *and* penetrate her wall of defenses. The few men who'd even tried had gone down to crashing defeat.

She knew she wasn't easy.

Her standards were very high.

She peeked over at Hunter, who was completely relaxed behind the wheel of the car.

What would her parents think of him?

What would Sophie think?

Her relatives?

Old beaux?

She smiled. Hunter Ashton was an old beau's nightmare. Maybe this weekend wouldn't be so bad, after all. In reality it was just one weekend out of her life and when it was over, her life would go on as before.

* * *

"Well, now I've done it," Hunter said, looking over at Noelle.

"What?"

He pointed to the Welcome to Missouri sign as they started across the bridge from Illinois. "I've taken you over the state line."

The words were no sooner out of his mouth than the limo conked out and coasted to a halt.

"I think you may have spoken too soon," Noelle said, as they sat in the dead car in the middle of the bridge above the Mississippi River. They weren't causing a traffic jam because traffic was light on a Thursday afternoon. But it wouldn't be long before there was one if Hunter didn't get the limo started.

"Come on, baby, start," Hunter coaxed, as he kept trying the ignition switch to no avail. His patience gone, he swore as he got out of the car to lift the hood.

Great, Noelle thought. The limo probably hadn't been rented out because it was a clunker. And now they were stranded in the middle of a bridge with people gawking as they drove around them.

Hunter returned to the limo.

"What's the verdict?"

"I've checked under the hood and everything looks okay to me. If I had to hazard a guess, I'd say the electronic modulator is out."

"Which means?"

"We need a tow truck."

Not exactly the entrance Noelle had planned.

"Hey, Noellie..." someone called from a Toyota Tercel sedan that passed them. The Toyota pulled over in front of them and stopped and a guy got out.

Oh, no, Noelle groaned to herself. No one worse could have stopped. It was Freddie Barton, of all people.

An old beau. And an old lover. Her first.

One who'd dumped her when one of her father's businesses had gone under. Now that her father was back on top, Noelle supposed Freddie had changed his tune. She was good enough to talk to again.

She'd be polite, but only because they needed a ride.

"Friend of yours?" Hunter asked, watching Freddie approach.

Freddie was short and dark, and thought he was handsome. You could tell by the swagger. What he was was cute—in a pesky sort of way. He had brown puppy-dog eyes and a great head of slicked-back hair.

As far as she was concerned, Freddie had never happened. She'd almost convinced herself of that. Almost forgotten the back seat of his Chevy. Unfortunately the twinkle in Freddie's eye said it had happened, and he hadn't forgotten.

Only she was the one who'd have to deal with the skeletons crawling out of her closet to meet her on the way home.

"He was once," she muttered, hating to admit to her bad judgment.

"*Good* friend?" Hunter prompted.

She didn't answer him.

Hunter slid down the window of the limo. "You look like the cavalry to me, man."

"Sure thing. Why don't we load you up in my car and we'll call for a tow truck on my car phone while I run you over to Noellie's parents'. You're here for the wedding, aren't you, Noellie?"

"You know about the wedding?" she asked, surprised.

"Heck, I'm in it. I'm the groom's cousin."

She'd forgotten. The scenario worsened. Not only was she at the wedding with a pretend date, Freddie was going to be there, too. All weekend, if he was a member of the wedding party. Great, just great.

"Well, *Noellie,* whatcha wanna do?" Hunter asked, teasing her with his killer grin.

"What I want to do isn't legal in this state," she retorted.

"Noellie!"

"Murder, I meant," she said, shoving open her door before Freddie came around to do it.

When they were all standing by the limo's trunk, Noelle made introductions.

"Aren't you dressed kinda casual for a limo driver?" Freddie asked Hunter as he shook his hand.

For the first time, Noelle read what was on Hunter's pink T-shirt. The pink color was due to the T-shirt having been washed with something red. The color was as tacky as the message on the T-shirt. You've Been a Naughty Girl—Go to My Room.

"I'm not the limo driver. I'm Noellie's date. I borrowed the limo."

"Quit calling me Noellie," Noelle said between clenched teeth.

Hunter just grinned at her as he opened the trunk of the limo and began lifting out their stuff; his bag, her suitcase, the wedding gift....

"Where's my dress?" Noelle cried out when she realized that it wasn't in the trunk of the car.

"What dress? You didn't bring any dress with you when you came down from your apartment. Your hands were full with the gift and your suitcase and your Popsicle stick."

"Oh, no! I let Barbara Ann get me so rattled that I left my perfect dress hanging in my bedroom. No, it was you with your honking—that's what got me so rattled. You're the reason I—"

"Now, sugar pie, don't be upset. You don't want Freddie here to see us quarrel, do you? I'm sure we can find you another perfect dress right here in St. Louis. A nice red one."

"Uh, cars are starting to pile up, we'd better get this show on the road and a tow truck called," Freddie interjected.

Hunter slammed the trunk closed and followed Freddie to his car, carrying the luggage and the wedding gift. Bringing up the rear, Noelle wondered how she could ever have liked Freddie. Comparing Hunter and Freddie showed Hunter in a much better light.

Hunter was taller, cuter, had some charm, and somehow she didn't think money was all that important to him. Wow, that was a first—her preferring a man to whom money wasn't important. Money was everything to Freddie. He would never have offered to buy her an awful red dress.

A tear slid down her cheek. She couldn't believe she'd left her perfect dress behind. And worse, she couldn't believe that she would be arriving for Sophie's wedding with a bought date and an old beau.

It didn't bode well for the weekend.

Freddie made the call for a tow truck, then turned to Noelle who'd dived into the back seat so she wouldn't have to sit next to Freddie. "So, what does your date do, if he's not a limo driver?"

Hunter didn't take offense. She didn't know what Hunter did, but she wasn't going to let Freddie get away with being the jerk he was.

"Hunter does well. *Very well.*"

Hunter chuckled in the front seat.

"How about you, Noellie? I hear you're doing real well for yourself in Chicago," Freddie said, his eyes back on the road. "Your mama said you worked at a bank. You already a head teller or something?"

"She's vice president. Vice president of Fidelity Trust," Hunter informed him. "How about you, Freddie? What do you do?"

"I've built a Toyota dealership into a real profitable little business. This baby is one of my brand-new models. What do you think of it, Noellie?"

Noelle didn't want to burst his bubble, but the Toyota, while impressive, had looked more like an economy car next to the white limo Hunter drove—even if the limo was borrowed.

"How's Sophie holding up? Last time I talked to her she had prewedding jitters. I hope after all the plans Mom and Dad have made, she doesn't leave Marky waiting at the altar."

"Not a chance. Cousin Marky's a catch. He works for me as a mechanic."

"Are you going to be at the rehearsal?" Noelle asked, hoping against hope he wasn't.

"I wouldn't miss it. The rehearsal dinner afterward is at Damon's. I've been hungry for barbecue ribs and onion loaf all week. Well, here we are, folks," Freddie said as they pulled into the long, winding drive that led to her parents' new home.

When the car stopped, Hunter got out and held the back door open for Noelle. As she slipped out of the car, she noticed Freddie watching them and impulsively threw her arms around Hunter's neck. The kiss she laid on the surprised Hunter was as salacious as she could make it and Hunter returned it in kind until she was weak in the knees.

"Wowie, Miss Noellie. I guess we're much better good friends than I thought," Hunter whispered beneath his breath when she broke away.

She glared at him.

"Oh, that was for ol' Freddie's benefit, wasn't it?" he said, as if he hadn't known it all along.

Noelle had to repress the urge to kick him in the shin. It would have given away the truth to Freddie. Although after that kiss, she wasn't sure just what the truth really was. In any case, Hunter Ashton knew his way around a salacious kiss.

When she didn't answer, Hunter persisted. "What the hell did Freddie do to you, anyway?"

"He dumped me, okay?"

"Noelle!" A younger, shorter version of Noelle came running from the house to embrace Noelle.

Where Noelle was racehorse sleek, Sophie still had some of her baby fat. Noelle's brown hair was discreetly sexy while Sophie's riot of red curls was outrageous.

"Guess I'll be going," Freddie said.

Hunter opened his wallet and pulled out a C-note. "Here's for your trouble. Now, if you'll open the trunk, I'll get our things."

Sophie and Noelle were chattering as Freddie drove away leaving Hunter standing with his arms full. "This suitcase of yours weighs a ton. What'd you do—bring work with you?"

Noelle's guilty look told him she had.

"Don't be silly. Noelle's going to be busy having a great time this weekend. Oh, we haven't met, have we? I'm Sophie, Noelle's baby sister."

Hunter took her offered hand and kissed it. "Hunter Ashton," he said, then looked to Noelle and added, "Noelle's very good friend."

"Noelle!"

"We're here to celebrate one wedding—yours, Sophie. Don't put any ideas into Mom and Dad's head, promise?"

"Okay, I'll behave, but you know Mom and Dad.... Wait till they see what a dishy guy you showed up with. I bet Freddie is spitting nails. Why did Freddie bring you, anyway?"

"The limo broke down on the bridge and we had to call a tow truck. Freddie came along and..." Noelle shrugged.

"Limo—"

"I thought maybe you could use an extra," Hunter said, winking.

"Wow, where did you two meet?" Sophie asked, impressed.

Noelle and Hunter looked at each other.

As Noelle remained speechless, Hunter answered, "We met at a hotel."

"Noelle!"

"It was a...ah...." Noelle began trying to explain.

"It was a charity function my sister organized," Hunter supplied.

"Well, come on inside before it starts getting crazy around here. Mom and Dad think they're marrying off a princess or something. The wedding has grown from an intimate dinner for friends to something I don't even want to think about. I'll get too nervous."

"You're going to make a beautiful bride," Hunter offered, "Just relax and enjoy your special day."

"I like this beau of yours, Noelle," Sophie said, grinning. "Why don't you take him upstairs to your new bedroom, Noelle, so you can freshen up before Mom and Dad get back from the florist's. It's the bedroom on the left at the top of the stairs."

Hunter followed Noelle upstairs with their luggage. Once they were inside the room he set down the luggage and went to test out the bed. Bouncing on it, he pronounced it to his liking.

"Come on over here, Noellie, and join me," he coaxed.

"No. And stop calling me Noellie, I told you. We're in my bedroom to freshen up, not for you to get fresh."

"Guess we're not such good friends behind closed doors, huh?"

"We're not going to be behind closed doors together. I'm sure there must be an extra bedroom for you somewhere in this big house."

"Now, Noellie, how would that look?"

"Like you're a gentleman and I'm a proper lady."

"Proper ladies don't know how to kiss like you do. Where'd you learn how? You got some sort of secret past you want to confess?"

"I was only acting for Freddie's benefit and you know it."

"Want to do some acting for my benefit . . . ?"

She threw her brush at him.

3

"But, Mother, I don't want—" Sophie broke off her complaint as Hunter and Noelle joined the family in the living room.

"Why hello, son." Noelle's father rose to his full six feet to offer his bear paw of a hand. "I'm Jack Perry." Noelle's father was a big imposing man with prematurely white hair. His dark brown eyes were as warm and friendly as his manner. "What's your handicap, son?"

"Excuse me?"

"Father's a golf nut," Noelle explained. "And don't get nervous, he calls everyone son."

Jack pulled the redhead beside him on the sofa to her feet and hugged her to him. "And this gorgeous lady is my wife, Grace."

"They're always necking. You'll get used to it," Noelle whispered, as Hunter took her mother's hand.

Noelle noticed how much her mother's taste in decor had changed since their last home. She'd changed from chrome-and-glass sleek to casual chic, by the look of the cushy white sofas with ruffled skirts fronting the oversize fireplace. Pickled wood floors and black-and-white photo prints were further evidence of her mother's change in taste.

"We're just having a little discussion here about a family custom Sophie's balking at," Jack said as they all settled on the sofas.

"I don't care what anyone says. I'm not agreeing to it. It's dumb," Sophie declared.

"It's a harmless family custom," Noelle said, trying to mediate.

"You wouldn't think so if it was you being kidnapped. I know you. You wouldn't have it."

"What are we talking about?" Puzzled, Hunter looked from one to another.

"They want to have me kidnapped at the wedding reception," Sophie complained, looking to someone outside the family for support.

"It sounds like a great adventure to me, Sophie. If you want, I'll even volunteer to be the one who comes to rescue you."

Sophie didn't brighten a watt. If anything, she looked even glummer.

"The groom has to be the one to rescue her, according to family custom," Noelle explained.

Hunter grinned. "Even better."

Jack planted a big kiss on Grace's cheek. "That's right. I rescued Grace—eventually we even made it back to the reception."

"But what if Marky won't pay the ransom to get me back? What if he gets cold feet or something?"

Grace reached over and patted Sophie's thigh. "Of course, Marky will pay to get you back. Don't talk such nonsense."

Sophie clearly wasn't convinced, for whatever reason.

"Come on, Sophie, we'll talk some more about this later," Jack coaxed. "Right now, I think we all should get acquainted with Noelle's new beau."

It was the part of coming home Noelle had been dreading ever since Hunter had got up at the bachelor auction to acknowledge he was the man she had bought. It would be just too embarrassing if anyone found out she'd had to buy a date for her baby sister's wedding.

"What do you do, son?"

"Father—"

"It's okay," Hunter assured her. "I do a little drawing...."

Yeah, unemployment, Noelle thought. He really should be in sales. He was certainly selling her family a bill of goods.

"Oh, an artist. How lovely," Grace said, her eyes approving. "I dabble at painting a little myself. Do you do portraits... still life... landscapes...?"

"What I do is more along the lines of fantasy...."

Noelle squirmed. Now was not the time for him to start being truthful.

Hunter looked at Sophie. "I draw a comic book," he said with a dismissive shrug. "Valerie Valor..."

"You're *him*. You're *that* Hunter Ashton!" Sophie cried, her dark eyes wide.

"'Fraid so."

When her parents and sister looked puzzled, Sophie went on to explain. "Valerie Valor, the Viking Princess of Venus—you know."

"Who?" Grace and Jack chorused.

"What!" Noelle looked at Hunter as if he'd grown three horns from the top of his head.

"Hunter's the guy who does the best superheroine comic book ever. Valerie Valor is so cool. She wears this red bustier and thigh-high boots while doing in the bad guys. All my friends just— Wait till they hear you're dating Hunter Ashton, Noelle! Why didn't you tell me?"

"Yes, *why* didn't you tell us?" Jack asked, suspicion in his eyes. "I thought Sophie said the two of you were—"

"It's my fault, sir," Hunter said, jumping in. "Obviously a bank vice-president isn't the comic-book-reading type. When I realized she didn't know what I did, I thought I'd keep it my secret for a while. It was refreshing not to have someone wanting me just because I was a celebrity of sorts. Noelle wanted me only for myself."

His shin wasn't handy so she ground her heel into his foot.

He swallowed his "Ouch!" almost inaudibly.

Grace nudged Jack and beamed at the smiling Hunter and blushing Noelle while Sophie went to answer the ringing telephone.

"You should have gone into sales, Hunter," Noelle muttered under her breath.

"I did," he whispered back, a cocky grin in his tone of voice. "You bought me, Noelle, remember?"

Sophie came running back into the room and threw herself at her father, sobbing.

"What's wrong, princess?" Jack asked, looking at Grace helplessly.

"My wedding is ruined!" Sophie cried.

"What are you talking about, Sophie? What's gone wrong?" Grace asked, rushing to console Sophie.

"I just...just talked to the singer for the band I—" she sniffed "—I hired for the wedding and... and..." She started crying again.

"What is it? What's wrong?" Noelle asked.

"They had a fight and broke up. Now I don't have music for my wedding," Sophie wailed.

"Don't cry, Sophie," Jack said, patting his daughter's head. "We'll think of something."

"Who's got a newspaper?" Hunter asked.

"The newspapers are in the basket there by the sofa," Grace said, pointing. "Why?"

"It's Thursday, there should be a listing of entertainment for the weekend, the names of local bands, where they might be playing."

"But I don't have time to look for another band," Sophie wailed. "I have a million things to take care of before the wedding."

"Don't worry, Noelle and I will take care of it," Hunter assured her, picking up the calendar section of the newspaper and scanning it.

"We will?" Noelle said, looking at him.

"Sure. Don't worry about the music. Noelle and I will find something for Saturday night, Sophie. Aha, here's what I was looking for. The Blue Shamrock is having open band auditions starting at two o'clock. Noelle and I will go check it out."

"But the rehearsal dinner is—"

"We'll be back in time," Hunter assured Grace.

Grabbing Noelle's arm, he ushered her outside.

"Do you really think we can—"

Hunter closed the door of the limo—which had been returned from the repair shop and was now running smoothly—and went around to the driver's side and got in, assuring her they'd find a band for Sophie's wedding. They drove in silence—a silence that was only punctuated by Noelle's directions on how to get to the Blue Shamrock. Hunter parked the limo and they went in.

Noelle was not impressed. The Blue Shamrock didn't look too promising. It was decorated in early rec room, with wood paneling and a gold-veined mirrored-tile wall behind the bar.

The band onstage was playing "Spanish Eyes" about one beat too slow and twenty years too late.

"I saw the limo outside, it must be Heartbreaker's," the burly, bold bartender said, taking their drink order.

"The limo is mine," Hunter explained. "What's a band like Heartbreaker doing here?"

"They're here to check out the drummer in Silver Moon, I heard."

The group onstage finished and a new band, carrying accordions and tubas, took their place. Soon oompah music filled the air.

"What do you think?" Hunter teased Noelle. "Do you think Sophie knows how to polka?"

"No. I sure hope the bands get better or we're wasting our time. We're never going to get a decent band at the last minute, Hunter."

"Oh, ye of little faith. I promised a band and I'll get one."

"I said a *decent* band, Hunter."

They endured the polka music played with more enthusiasm than skill. Even though Noelle didn't believe Hunter's promise to find a band, still, she found it very endearing that he was trying.

"Ah, here's something a little more contemporary," Hunter said when the polka band finally finished and new musicians took their place.

"You've got to be kidding."

"What? You don't think Sophie would like them?" Hunter pretended disbelief, his wiseass grin giving him away.

"I hardly think it's any girl's dream to have the band of an Elvis impersonator play at her wedding."

Hunter clutched at his heart as if she'd wounded him to the quick. "Don't be cruel, Miss Noelle."

"Hey, Heartbreaker's here. The bartender wasn't just kidding around. That's Blake Penny at the door," Noelle said, pointing.

Hunter looked around. "You're right. Order me another drink, will you? I'll be right back." With that, Hunter got up and left the table to walk over to where Blake Penny stood talking to the owner of the Blue Shamrock.

Well, Hunter wasn't shy, she'd give him that. And a lot more, if pressed, she thought, acknowledging the strong physical attraction between them. Hunter wasn't the serious kind of guy you made long-range plans with but he sure was a fun date. And a considerate one.

Not many hired dates would try to scare up a band at the last minute for a wedding.

As she watched the Elvis impersonator sing in a white studded jumpsuit, she wondered why all the Elvis impersonators played Elvis in his later years. She had the feeling an impersonator of a young, hunky Elvis would clean up.

Hunter returned to the table a few minutes later when the Elvis band was finished with its audition.

"Silver Moon is up next," he told Noelle. "I understand they're pretty good."

"Maybe we can hire them for the wedding, then," Noelle said, brightening. "I hate to go back home without a band to replace the one that canceled out on Sophie."

"Oh, we won't disappoint Sophie. She's going to have a wedding to remember. Everyone will be talking about it for a long time, I promise."

Noelle carefully studied Hunter. "I don't mean talking about a ridiculous band," she warned, just in case Hunter had any crazy ideas. So far they hadn't seen a band she'd even remotely consider. A boom box would be preferable.

Surprisingly the next sounds from the stage were fabulous. Silver Moon was a talented band. They played a medley that displayed their versatility.

"We've got to get them!"

Hunter smiled at the excitement in Noelle's voice. He'd like to see more of it. It was obvious to him that she exerted a great deal of effort clamping down on her natural enthusiasm. She kept a tight rein on herself. But every so often he glimpsed the unrestrained

Noelle . . . and he wanted her to come out and play—with him. This weekend he planned to see what he could do to coax her out.

"The drummer is really good. I can see why Heartbreaker is thinking about recruiting him," Hunter agreed.

They weren't the only ones applauding when Silver Moon finished.

"Go talk to them," Noelle urged as they were packing up their instruments to go offstage. "And try to keep their price reasonable. I don't want Mother and Father to go broke."

Hunter got up and went over to the stage just as Blake Penny did.

Noelle nervously watched the two men talking to the band members of Silver Moon. It seemed to take forever for Hunter to return to the table.

"Well?" she asked hopefully.

Hunter shook his head no.

"Why not?"

"They've got a gig. They're playing here on Saturday night."

"Oh."

Noelle frowned. "I told you we're not going to get a band. It's hopeless. Sophie's wedding is going to be ruined."

"There're still three more bands to audition," Hunter said, reasonably.

Noelle finished the drink she'd been nursing and glumly watched a new band take the stage. The musicians' dreadlocks and hip-hop clothes indicated they played rap.

"I think you need another drink," Hunter said, signaling the bartender. "You've got to have faith in me."

The band did a cover of a Snoop Doggy Dogg tune and Noelle rolled her eyes at Hunter. "I don't think my father would be able to two-step to this, do you, Hunter?"

"Maybe the next band," Hunter agreed.

The next band was rock and roll.

"Do you think teeth can rattle?" Hunter asked when they turned up their amps.

The last band was Three Jacks and a Queen. The jacks were in their eighties with the queen probably a young seventy-five.

"Got any more ideas?" Noelle asked Hunter, her tone of voice informing him that if he did, she didn't want to hear them.

"I guess it's the boom box, then. Sophie is going to be so disappointed. She really thought you could pull off coming up with a band."

Just then Blake Penny came up to their table. "Gotta leave, man," he said to Hunter.

"Blake, this is Noelle Perry. Noelle, this is Blake Penny," Hunter said.

"Uh, hi," Noelle said, tongue-tied. Unlike Hunter, she couldn't make friends with a celebrity at the drop of a hat.

"Perry?" Blake Penny repeated. "Is this pretty lady any relation to the bride?"

"Noelle is Sophie's sister, and my date for the wedding," Hunter answered.

"You ought to hang on to him," Blake said. "The man has good taste in bands and women. Well, I'll be seeing you." Blake Penny left them to have a final word with the drummer in Silver Moon. Noelle gazed at Hunter in puzzlement.

"How did he know Sophie's name?"

"I told him."

"Oh."

Hunter paid their bar tab and left a healthy tip. "Come on, we'd better get back," he said, looking at his watch. "The rehearsal is in an hour."

As they left the Blue Shamrock, Noelle persisted, "Why did you tell Blake Penny Sophie's name?"

Hunter held open the door of the limo. "It seemed like a good idea," he said, adding, "since Heartbreaker is going to be playing at Sophie's wedding."

"What?"

"Heartbreaker is going to play at your sister's wedding."

"That's impossible."

"Why?"

"Because first, Heartbreaker has a hit album out and must be booked, and even if they did have an open date, my parents could never afford—"

"I took care of it."

"But I can't let you—"

"Sure, you can. Don't worry. Blake Penny is a huge fan of Valerie Valor's. All it cost me is an autographed original strip."

"But that must be worth—"

"A wedding gig. Just say, 'Thank you, Hunter.'"

She reached up and did just that with another one of her surprising kisses. The kind she'd laid on him for Freddie's benefit when they'd first arrived. Only this time it was for his benefit.

"You're very welcome," he said, breaking off the kiss before he did something foolish.

When they arrived at the Perrys' home and told Sophie the news, she kissed him, too. About a hundred times in succession.

And then she was on the phone calling everyone.

He was everyone's hero before the wedding even began.

An hour later they all rode to the rehearsal in the white limo. On the way out, Jack Perry had grabbed a bottle of champagne from the fridge and was passing the bottle. While he and Grace continued their discussion with Sophie about the family custom of kidnapping the bride at the wedding reception, Noelle turned her thoughts to Hunter Ashton and Valerie Valor.

He spent his days with a cartoon heroine who ran around rescuing people, dressed in a red bustier and thigh-high boots. Hunter dealt in fantasy, all right.

He was a fantasy.

Her kind of fantasy man.

Suddenly she had the strongest desire to have an adventurous fling with Hunter, a fling that would last as long as the wedding weekend and no longer.

Who would know—what could it hurt—if for just one weekend she gave in to impulse? No one in the banking community would ever know. Her conservative-banker image would remain intact.

Hunter gave her a wink before leaning his head against the door and napping, tired, no doubt, from a sleepless night and the long drive.

Noelle continued to study him as he napped.

Hunter Ashton was as tempting as they came. Springs of blond hair curled in the vee of his dark polo shirt. On the drive from Chicago she'd noticed how the sun glinted on his bare arms, giving him an almost-golden glow. Making him look like a wicked angel.

How would it feel to run her hands over...? What no one knew or even suspected was how similar she was to the rest of her loony family—or would be, if she allowed herself to give in to her wild inclinations.

What was stopping her was her awareness of just the sort of trouble giving in to her desires could lead to. And unlike her parents and sister, she wasn't cut out to live in constant turmoil. She hadn't thrived on the continual upheaval the way the rest of the family had.

But maybe she had gone a little overboard in protecting herself from herself. The real reason she hadn't dated much was because the men who appealed to her in truth were a lot like Hunter Ashton.

She was drawn to men who were unconventional and who were effortlessly sexy.

Men who were uncontrollable.

Trouble.

Unsettling.

And unsafe.

But, hey, she wasn't making a lifetime commitment, here. This was just a weekend out of town. It would be like one of those vacation shipboard ronances. They'd have some fun, part, and neither of them would be hurt by the experience.

A little fun never hurt anyone.

Hunter Ashton wasn't napping.

He was thinking.

And knew Noelle Perry would be surprised at his thoughts.

When he'd begun the trip to St. Louis with Noelle he'd thought of it as an adventure. He liked feeling a part of a family. Maybe Daphne was right. Maybe he did need to get out more. His usual method of operation was to bury himself in his projects and then have a week or two of what Daphne referred to as "wreck-eation" that involved a meaningless fling with a willing woman.

Maybe, at twenty-eight, he needed more stability in his life. His career was firmly established and money would never be a problem. But the way he was living wasn't very healthy—physically or emotionally.

This time, he was going to take it slow and see if it developed into something more than a slap and a tickle. Not that there was anything wrong with slap and tickle...

"What are you smiling at?" Noelle demanded to know, nudging his knee with her foot from where she sat across the seat.

He opened one eye.

"I was thinking about shopping for a red dress with you for the wedding. When do you think you'd have time for a little shopping spree?"

"I'm not buying red. And I'm not going with you. I can shop for my own clothes. I'm a grown-up girl, you know."

"I've noticed," he said, popping open his other baby blue and surveying her. "Size ten, right?"

"How do you—"

"My sister, Daphne is a size ten. I go shopping with her all the time. She thinks I have great taste."

She'd responded negatively to his proposal of a shopping spree out of habit. Actually, a shopping spree would be fun. A new experience. She'd never had a man shop with her or for her before.

"Okay," she agreed. "Maybe tomorrow morning when the stores open we can hit Plaza Frontenac or the Galleria."

"What time do the stores open?" Hunter asked, considering.

"Nine-thirty, ten..."

"I have a golf game."

"I should have known. Don't play him for money. And I should warn you he likes to look for golf balls when he plays, which means it will take you until at least three."

"Let's plan to shop at four. That will give me time to shower and we can catch a bite to eat before I have to go to the bachelor party, according to your father."

"There really is a bachelor party?"

"Your father arranged it."

Noelle just shook her head. Some weekend "fling" this was going to be. Hunter would have to schedule her in between *his* social engagements.

*   *   *

The minister kept looking at his watch.

Sophie kept looking at the door.

Jack and Grace kept looking at his other.

As did Hunter and Noelle.

The looks between Grace and Jack were looks of parental concern. Grace made mention of "all that potato salad."

The looks between Hunter and Noelle were inappropriate, considering the situation. Noelle knew it full well. They had a possible crisis on their hands. Marky was late for the wedding rehearsal. Not a good sign. Especially with what seemed to be a skittish bride. Sophie was nothing if not a volatile teenager. Her mother was right—there was "all that potato salad."

And all Noelle could think about was seducing Hunter as soon as possible, as often as possible.

Hunter, for his part, looked as though he was enjoying every aspect of the evening's prospects.

"We'll have to begin," the minister said, his words echoing in the massive empty church and focusing all thoughts on how to conduct a wedding rehearsal without the groom. "I can't wait any longer. I have another rehearsal scheduled in half an hour that I must get to. Someone will have to stand in for the—"

There was a crash of the heavy wooden entry door as it was shoved open, and a young man entered the church, running.

"Marky, where have you been?" Sophie demanded to know.

"At the hospital. Freddie fell off the loading dock and broke his leg. He's going to be all right, but we're going to have to find a replacement for him. Okay, let's get started."

"Is he always so pale?" Hunter asked Noelle, as they stood on the sidelines and watched the bridesmaids and groomsmen assemble and go through the trial run for Saturday's wedding.

"I shouldn't think so," Noelle answered, "but I can't say for sure, as I've never met him."

"It's a whirlwind courtship, then? That explains some of your sister's nervousness."

"Brides are always nervous."

"I thought that was grooms."

"What does a groom have to be nervous about? All he has to do is show up."

"Exactly."

Noelle shoved her elbow into his ribs.

"Will you quit beating me up? If I'd known how physical you were, I'd have demanded combat—"

"Shh..." Grace shushed them, as Marky and Sophie went through their vows.

"Okay, I think that about covers it," the minister said, wrapping up. "I'll see you all on Saturday. Don't forget the rings." With that, the portly man snapped his Bible shut and scurried down the aisle for the exit.

"Okay, everyone. It's barbecue ribs and onion loaf at Damon's on South Lindbergh. Drive carefully," Jack said, organizing the rehearsal dinner. "Oh, it's outside in the garden, don't forget."

"Can one hope that's a beer garden?" Hunter inquired.

"I do like your young man," Jack said, capturing Hunter in a bear hug. "We're going to ride to Damon's with Marky's parents, Noelle. We're still haggling over who's gonna cough up for the open bar and how open the bar is going to be. We'll see you there. And, Hunter, have a cold one waiting for me, okay?"

"Yes, sir." As they watched everyone pile into their cars and Sophie into Marky's clunker, Hunter stated the obvious. "I guess it's just you and me in the limo."

"Good, I've always wanted to see what it felt like to sit in the back of one."

"Noelle, they're expecting us to be at the rehearsal dinner—Jack's expecting his cold beer to be waiting for him.... Okay, okay, don't kick me. I get it. You want me to drive."

They ended up in the front seat together.

Noelle rationalized it was because she didn't want anyone to think there was anything strange about their relationship.

"Do me a favor, would you?" she asked when they were on the road."

"If you promise not to hit or kick me."

"I'm serious, Hunter. I want you to quit being so perfect. My father is going to get attached to you and ask me all kinds of questions when you don't show up my next trip back home."

"It makes me wonder what kind of men you've been bringing home."

"You're the first," she reluctantly admitted.

"No wonder they're so happy to see me."

"Just drive, Hunter."

"Yes, ma'am."

In the lush garden adjacent to the restaurant, a long table was set up with white balloons attached to each of the chairs. Several bottles of champagne stood on the table. A water fountain, in the center of the garden, lent a festive atmosphere to the evening. After the wedding party was seated, a waiter began serving barbecue ribs, coleslaw and baked beans.

Marky and Sophie seemed to have settled their differences.

Both sets of parents were beaming.

The wedding party was flirting and popping balloons once the meal was over.

A string quartet that had been playing in the restaurant, came into the garden to play a romantic ballad for the engaged couple and a special piece for Grace from Jack.

Despite Noelle's request, Hunter went on being perfect.

Just before the dinner broke up, Marky was called to the phone.

"Did you tell her?" a male voice demanded.

"Not yet," Marky said loudly into the phone, and then guiltily looked around. He was relieved that no one from the wedding party was in listening distance.

"You are going to tell her, aren't you?"

"Yes," Marky whispered.

"See that you do."

Marky flinched at the sound of the phone receiver being slammed down. He gently hung up his phone, and with a sigh, he turned and went back to join the wedding party.

4

"Who wants a piece of my caramel-pecan apple pie?" Grace asked when she and Jack arrived home just after Hunter and Noelle did. Sophie and Marky had gone out on the town with the rest of the wedding party.

"Not me, dear," Jack said. "I'll just have one of your sticky sweet kisses to tide me over until morning." He pulled Grace into his arms and stole one. "I'm going up to bed," he announced, upon releasing Grace. "Don't forget we've got a golf game in the morning, son."

"I won't," Hunter promised.

"Count me out, too," Noelle said, unsuccessfully trying to stifle a yawn. "All that food has made me sleepy. I'm turning in early, too."

Grace looked at Hunter. "You aren't going to make me eat alone, are you, dear?"

"You know, I might just have an inch of space left for something sweet."

He followed Grace out to the greenhouse kitchen and took a seat at the square oak table cluttered with R.S.V.P. cards and mail.

Grace took the pie from the refrigerator and sliced generous pieces for both of them. Then she heated the slices in the microwave before adding scoops of French vanilla ice cream atop them.

She set the pieces of pie on the table and poured each of them a cold glass of milk before taking a seat at the table.

While Hunter savored the pie and ice cream, Grace sorted through the day's mail, adding a tardy wedding R.S.V.P. to the pile for the final count for the wedding-reception dinner.

"Great pie, Grace," Hunter said, as she slit open the tab from the credit-card company.

Grace frowned at the bottom line on her credit-card statement. "I'll sell you the recipe for twenty grand. Jack would stroke out if he knew how much money I've spent on this wedding. The potato salad alone—"

"Surely Jack knows how much," Hunter said, as Grace toyed with her slice of pie.

Grace shook her head no. "Jack's trouble is he can't say no—to me, to his daughter, his friends, himself. And he doesn't like to be bothered with mundane things. Unlike Noelle, keeping track of money bores him."

Hunter polished off the last bit of his pie. He licked his lips to show appreciation and got a smile from Grace. "So then you're the one who worries, is that it, Grace?"

Grace looked a little remorseful, then shook her head. "I'm afraid I'm not much better than Jack. I only worry when the statement comes at the end of the month. I must admit, shopping is a great mood booster. There's just something about buying that gives you a little thrill, you know what I mean?''

Hunter had the distinct feeling he was talking to a shopaholic. No wonder Noelle was so conservative. Someone had to be responsible and she'd been elected a long time ago by her family. Jack and Grace were charming, but irresponsible. Sophie was, after all, only a kid who thought the world revolved around her—as most teenagers did.

He supposed in a way he'd shoved his twin sister, Daphne, into that same role. More so since their parents had died in a boating accident when they were in college.

Well, people could change. He was prepared to demonstrate to Noelle that he was not some loony cartoonist. He'd be a perfect gentleman all weekend. There would be plenty of time when they were back in Chicago for him to see if anything would come of this humming attraction he'd felt between them right from the start.

This weekend he'd concentrate on working on Jack and Grace so he'd be invited back to visit. Winning them over couldn't hurt his cause. And Sophie was already on his side, having immediately been taken by the fact of him being *the* Hunter Ashton.

Yes, being a perfect gentleman was just the ticket.

"Well, Grace, you be sure and let me know if you need a loan. It'll be just between the two of us," he said with a wink as he stood to go upstairs to collect his stuff and put it in another bedroom.

"Don't tempt me," she said, waving him off and stacking the R.S.V.P. cards into tidy piles of twenty-five for a final tabulation.

"Who do you think you're kidding, Hunter?"

"You know, Valerie, most comic-book characters don't risk giving their creators grief." Hunter started up the stairs.

"Yeah, but *you* a perfect gentleman? I know you want Noelle bad." Valerie fell in step beside him.

"So do I, believe me. That's why I'm moving my stuff to an empty bedroom. That way I won't be tempted. Great plan, don't you think?"

"You're forgetting something—there's a flaw in your 'great' plan," Valerie argued, as Hunter continued upstairs to the second floor.

"What's that?" he asked, sticking his head in an open bedroom and turning on the light. "Oh yeah, now I remember."

The bedroom—like all the others he'd made a casual perusal of earlier in the day—was filled with wedding presents and decorations for the reception at the country club.

"It doesn't matter," he assured himself and Valerie. "We can share a bedroom without—"

"Sure, you can...."

"Valerie—"

"Yes?"

"I'm going shopping tomorrow with Noelle to find her something to wear to the wedding. I *was* planning to look around for a new outfit for you as well, while

I was at it. I thought I might even get Noelle's input.
But since you seem bent on annoying me . . ."

"Okay, okay. I believe you can share a bedroom
with Noelle and remain a perfect gentleman. What else
would anyone expect from a man who allows himself
to be sold at a bachelor auction?"

"It was for a good cause."

"Right."

"I can behave. In fact, I promised Daphne that I
would."

"Right."

"I'm promising you right now. I will go knock on
Noelle's bedroom door. And when she lets me in I will
be a perfect gentleman."

"I believe you. And stay away from Victoria's Secret tomorrow. I want something sporty, nothing remotely like lingerie."

Hunter turned off the light and walked down the
hall to Noelle's bedroom. Valerie believed him, so why
didn't he believe himself? he wondered as he raised his
hand to knock on her bedroom door.

"Come in," she called out.

He took a deep breath and went inside.

It was pitch-dark. She'd turned off the light and
gone to bed already, if not to sleep. That would make
it easier. He'd just get undressed in the dark, hug his
edge of the bed and sleep like a baby till morning.

"Lock the door."

He was hearing things.

"Lock the door," Noelle repeated.

He did as she asked and reached to turn on the light.

"Don't turn on the light."

"O-kay." He lowered his hand to his side, waiting, desperately trying to adjust his eyes to seeing in the dark of the bedroom.

"Do you like me, Hunter?"

"Ah, sure." Why the hell was he so nervous? He turned in the direction of Noelle's voice and was just beginning to make out where she sat on the bed when she shoved back the sheet and got up.

"Do you like me enough, Hunter?" she asked, walking toward him wearing what sounded like satin and looked in the dark like boxer pajamas.

"Enough..." he repeated, clearing his throat.

"I like you, Hunter. I like you a real lot. Do you mind if I show you how much?"

"Um...n-no." He was dreaming. He'd fallen asleep eating pie at the kitchen table.

She reached out to place her hand on his cheek.

No. He wasn't asleep. He was awake. Fully awake. Bright-eyed and bushy-tailed, as a matter of fact. He could hear his own breathing in the silent, suddenly airless room.

Her thumb trailed over his lips.

He grabbed her hand, stilling it.

"You aren't going to chicken out on me, are you, Hunter? It's okay, you know. I know you prefer to deal with fantasy women. I'm not here to complicate your life. Or mine."

"What...what, ah... What are you here to do, Noelle?" He could see her now; his eyes had adjusted to the darkness of the bedroom. She wet her lips nervously.

"You aren't the only one weddings make horny, Hunter. So I thought, why not?"

"Why not, what—" He wanted to be sure. Jack Perry was a very big man. And even with her parents' bedroom being on the first level, below them ...

"Have a weekend fling. No strings. We both go back to the city and our own lives. Admit it. It's what you've had on your mind, anyway."

"I'd made up my mind I was going to be a perfect gentleman on the way up the stairs. I thought that was what you wanted."

"I changed my mind." She turned her head, pressing her lips to the back of his hand. "Is that a problem?" she murmured, licking his thumb.

"Noelle, honey, you can do whatever you please."

She brushed her body against his erection straining behind the fly of his dress slacks.

"Oh, yes, please!" Hunter rasped. His thigh muscles tightened instinctively when he slammed his mouth against her lush lips. As she leaned into him fully, returning his kiss, eager and hot, he tightly embraced her and slid his own hands over her satin-clad bottom to urge her even closer against him.

While they continued to frantically kiss, Noelle tugged at Hunter's polo shirt. Freeing it from his slacks, she pulled it over his head with a sense of urgency, and ran her soft hands over the thick hair covering his chest.

Hunter then took her hands in his, stilling them, and captured her lips in a drugging kiss.

Then, with a groan, he released her. "Jeez, I love an aggressive woman."

"Why? 'Cause you're a lazy man?" she teased.

"Lazy? I'll show you 'lazy,' woman. Take off my pants and I'll show you—"

Her hand went for his belt buckle.

His went for the satin-covered buttons of her pajama top. Clearly he knew his way around a button better than she knew her way around a buckle. He lowered his head, his mouth covering the nipple of her exposed breast.

He felt her fingertips clench the waistband of his slacks. She shuddered, a small moan escaping her lips when he began to lave the smooth coolness of her breasts, warming them until the peaks tightened.

Losing rein on his passion, he thrust a hand beneath the hem of her boxer pajama bottom to cup her warm, moist heat. He squeezed and released until she cried out and began working at his belt buckle with renewed urgency. Unfastening it, she slid it from the loops and let it slip to the floor.

"Careful, you'd better let me take it from here," he said, reluctantly moving his hands to undo the button of his slacks and gingerly inch down the zipper.

"Hurry," she urged.

"Greedy little thing, aren't you, Miss Noellie."

"Don't—"

"I know, I know." He dropped the "Noellie" and his pants at the same time.

"Uh-oh, looks like we've got us a problem here," he said, looking back and forth between them.

"What are you talking about?"

It was hard to keep the grin from his voice. "Well, since we're both wearing boxer shorts...I'm confused."

"So am I. What are you talking about?"

"Who gets on top—"

She tucked her fingertips inside the waistband of her satin boxers and slid them down her hips to her feet and swiftly kicked them aside. A tight, daring smile played on her lips.

"Still confused?"

"I'm speechless."

"Good."

He shed his boxers in a heartbeat and for the next ten minutes they came together fast and furious. Her bites at his neck were followed by a nibbling forage of his jawline. When he lifted her astride him, her hands clutched his hair. Moving so that she was braced against the wall, they took what they wanted from each other.

Selfishly.

Deliciously.

Both of them buried their mouths against each other to keep their cries of ecstasy from summoning her father with shotgun in hand.

Wonderfully saturated, the two slid down the wall together in a limp, sweaty tangle. His legs had turned to jelly, but he'd managed to pull her on top of him to cushion her descent to the floor.

After a moment he felt her fingers at his lips.

"What?" he asked, kissing them.

"I just knew I would feel you grinning."

"That's because I always grin when I'm happy."

"Not bad for a start," she said with a laugh.

"*Start?*"

"Are you telling me that's it? I thought you were *the* Hunter Ashton."

"I draw 'super' characters. *I'm* not one."

"Coulda fooled me."

"You do know how to encourage a fellow," Hunter said, glancing down for signs of life.

"I can be more encouraging," Noelle said, sliding down the length of him until her head rested at his groin.

"I've changed my mind."

She looked up, stopping her "encouragement."

"No, don't stop. How much champagne did you drink tonight, anyway?"

"Just enough," she informed him saucily, as she went back to encouraging him.

He certainly wasn't going to argue with that. Not when the result felt so, ah . . . sinfully good.

He told himself he was going to let her encourage him to hell and back.

He told himself he could handle anything she could dish out.

He was up for her. He chuckled to himself.

And then he bit his lip, overcome by the exquisite sensation.

"Noelle, honey," he breathed on a strangled groan, his hands cupping her head.

When he caught his breath and his eyes fluttered open, he saw that she had her head propped up on her elbow as she watched him.

"I, ah . . ." he began. He couldn't believe he'd . . .

"Guess I was a little too encouraging, huh?"

She giggled.

He laughed.

She got the giggles.

And suddenly he was kissing her.

And suddenly nothing was funny anymore.

They broke apart, both startled by the spontaneous real emotion. True feelings were frighteningly intimate.

And all at once they were shy with each other.

She reached for her pajama top.

He faked a yawn. "Guess we better hit the sheets. I have to get up early to play golf with your father."

"Me, too," Noelle said, trying to make conversation to hide the awkwardness between them. "I mean, I need to get some sleep, too. I have to go with Sophie and Mother in the morning to check out the last-minute details for the wedding. And then you have to power-shop with me tomorrow afternoon."

Hunter eased his body up. "That's right. I have to buy you that red dress I promised you."

"You've got to rent a tuxedo tomorrow, too. I can't believe you let Mother talk you into filling in for Freddie in the wedding party. Only Freddie would wind up in the hospital with a broken leg two days before a wedding."

"You going to go sign his cast?"

"No, I'd be too tempted to break his other leg."

"I'll remember not to piss you off. If I'm not giving you what you paid for, you be sure and tell me."

The look on her face was stricken. He'd said the worst thing he could say. He hadn't meant it like that.

And worse, there was nothing he could say that would take it back. Any attempt to make it better would only make it worse.

She scooped up her boxer sorts, pulled them on and dived beneath the sheet on the bed. Her body language said it all, making him feel like an even worse jerk. She was curled in the fetal position, her back to his side of the bed.

He slept in the nude. Normally it didn't chill him. But as he lay beside her, hugging the edge of the bed, he was cold.

Sleep was impossible.

"A perfect gentleman, huh?" Valerie said, intruding on his brooding.

"Go away."

"Oh, no, this is too good."

"Don't rub it in."

"Why don't you apologize to her?" she asked.

"It'll only make it worse."

"You mean you don't have the guts, Hunter."

"Go away."

"You're not going to let her spend the weekend thinking that you didn't feel anything—that tonight was just a performance of your duties as a weekend escort."

"How do you know it wasn't? She seduced me, you know. I really did plan to be a perfect gentleman—whether you believe it or not, Valerie."

"I've been there when you've been performing, just going through the motions between projects. I've been there when the women really didn't mean anything. This was different. You actually felt something. And when you begin to feel something you run like hell back inside yourself. You're a coward, Hunter Ashton.''

"And you're pushing it, Valerie. I'm sure they must have erasers around here somewhere," he threatened.

"You can rub me out, Hunter, but you can't erase the mistake you're making with Noelle."

"I'm not making a mistake." He wrapped the sheet around him tighter. "Leave me alone. I need to get some sleep so I can beat Jack's pants off him in the morning."

"I'd let Jack win if I were you. Okay, I'll leave you alone, if that's what you really want. It won't help you go to sleep, though. You're going to stay awake. Your conscience is going to bug you."

"*You* are my conscience."

"Right. I forgot. As I was saying, if you were the superhero Noelle thought you were, you'd apologize to her right now."

"She's sleeping."

"And you're dreaming."

"Well, I'm not the superhero she thought I was, okay?"

"Tell me about it. And here I thought Peter Pan was growing up."

"Shut up, Tinker Bell."

She was an idiot.

Noelle lay quietly beside Hunter, not moving a muscle. She didn't want him to know she hadn't fallen asleep. She wanted him to think that she'd been able to seduce him without another thought. Wanted him to think his careless words hadn't stung her.

What had started out as a lighthearted romp had become dangerously intimate when they'd connected through shared laughter.

Who would have thought an act of desperation—buying a male for sale at a bachelor auction—would have brought her someone she could really *like*?

If she were looking for someone she could truly like—which she wasn't.

Hunter Ashton wasn't looking for a relationship any more than she was.

This was a weekend fling.

Hunter was a date, nothing more. And she planned to get her money's worth. Plumping her pillow, she settled in for some very good dreams.

"What do you think of Noelle's young man?" Grace asked when she'd joined Jack in their big pine four-poster bed.

"I'll tell you tomorrow after we play golf," Jack mumbled sleepily.

"I like him."

"But then you never were a very good judge of men," he said on a chuckle. "If you were, you'd have taken your parents' advice and married that lawyer you were dating when you met me. He had great prospects. I didn't even have a job."

"I didn't fall in love with the lawyer. I fell in love with you."

"Much to your parents' chagrin."

"But not to mine," Grace assured him, snuggling up close.

"Did Sophie come home yet?" he asked, nuzzling Grace's ear.

"Not yet. You've got to stop worrying about her, Jack. She's going to be a married woman."

"You're a married woman and I worry about you," he countered. "Now, are you going to tell me how much this wedding is costing us, or am I going to have to pry that out of you?"

"My lips are sealed," Grace said with a giggle.

"We'll just see about that."

"Jack!"

"Why don't you want me to talk to her?" Sophie demanded. "She wants to talk to me."

"We've been over this before, Sophie," Marky said, exasperation in his voice. "Polly is an old girlfriend. She is jealous of you and doesn't want us to get married."

"Why didn't you tell me about her?"

"Look," Marky said, running his hands over the steering wheel as they sat outside Sophie's house in his car. "Polly will only try to come between us. She's a head case. Just ignore the notes she's been sending you. I'll deal with her."

"Well, I don't like it."

"Neither do I, but there's nothing I can do about it for the moment. Once we're married she'll give up on trying to get me back."

Sophie looked at her ring in the moonlight that filtered into the car. "I love my ring."

"It isn't very big."

"I don't care."

"But I do. I want my wife to have—"

"It doesn't matter, Marky. We've been rich and we've been poor. My mom and dad never let money—"

"Rich is better," Marky declared.

"Kiss me good-night, Marky," she said, changing the subject. She knew there was no changing his mind once he made it up.

When the kiss ended, Sophie said dreamily, "Just think, Marky, in only one day I'm going to be Mrs. Marky Bergen." She pushed open the car door to go inside.

"Remember what I said. Stay away from Polly," Marky warned.

"All right, all right. I will."

5

The golf course at the country club where Sophie was to have her wedding reception the next night was one of the best in St. Louis. Old money had laid out the manicured grounds and new money kept them clipped and green. That and chemicals.

Something about the dead calm of the golf course unnerved Hunter. There wasn't a bird chirp, a scurrying chipmunk or the flitting color of a butterfly anywhere. The wildlife paid a handsome price for all the dark green carpeting of the sculptured grounds.

This was no Disneyesque perfect picture, but a chilling picture of environmental irresponsibility. A picture of something that looked pleasant, but wasn't. Maybe this was a subject for Valerie Valor to tackle in his next project.

"Does the comic-book business pay well, son?" Jack Perry asked, interrupting Hunter's thoughts as he stopped the golf cart at the second hole of the course.

Hunter smiled to himself. Jack Perry not only looked like a big bear, he was a protective papa bear with his family. He was giving Hunter the "Are your intentions honorable, young man?" speech. *Were* his intentions honorable? They had been when he'd started up to Jack's daughter's room last night.

But lust had overpowered his best intentions. The match hadn't even gone one round. The song went, "Turn out the lights, the party's over..." But at last night's "Turn out the lights," the party had only just begun.

"I do all right," Hunter said modestly, watching Jack slice a drive down the fairway way to the left of the green.

Hunter sliced a drive straight and true to the green, eliciting a frown from Jack. The frown brought to mind Noelle's advice to let her father win. What the heck, he'd vowed to be a good guest. By the end of the second-hole play, Jack took a score of par and Hunter was one under par.

Jack's spirits had improved tremendously. "Bad luck on that hole, son. But don't worry, you're catching on real well. You know I bet you'd be a good golfer if you took a few lessons with the club pro and applied yourself. Golf is a game of concentration."

Concentration. If that was the case, Hunter knew he might as well hang it up for the day. He couldn't have concentrated on anything but Jack's daughter, Noelle, if his life had depended upon it. Last night had been amazing.

The sex had been ... the best. But it wasn't the sex that had him unable to concentrate. It was Noelle. There was something about her that had gotten under his skin. He'd almost woken her first thing this morning. But he hadn't because she'd been hurt by his words when they'd gone to bed and he didn't know how to make it right.

"How is Noelle really doing in Chicago?" Jack questioned. "Is she happy with her job? I think she spends too much time working. She was always such a serious child. I hope you can lighten her up, show her life can be fun."

"I'm doing my best, sir."

"It's your turn to putt, son. Try to keep your shoulders straight. You'll find you have more control of your ball that way."

Hunter sent his ball within inches of the third hole.

"See, what did I tell you? Yes, sir. I think I may have found me a golfing buddy."

"What about Marky, sir?"

"Even I know *that's* not going to last."

Hunter couldn't say that he could argue with Jack. "Then, how come—"

"Sophie's eighteen. She's my baby and she's got her heart set on marrying the guy. What if I'm wrong? What if she never forgave me?"

"It's pretty tough being a father, I guess."

"You'll find out, son. You'll find out. Take my advice and have sons."

They finished the third hole and Hunter drove them in the cart to the dog-legged hole four.

Jack stepped up to the tee and sailed one wide into the woods. "Wait here," Jack said, indicating a wooden bench. "I'm going to look for my ball."

Hunter sat down on the bench knowing it would be a while, as Noelle had forewarned him about Jack's expeditions into the woods. Some people just had a thing about finding free golf balls. Even people who spent thousands of dollars to belong to a private club.

"Did you hear that, Hunter?" Valerie taunted, practicing her golf swing with one of his woods. "Guess whose sons ol' Jack wants you to have?"

"Don't you ever give it a rest? The project is over. I told you to take a vacation. Be a pal, Valerie, and take a hike."

"Don't be getting all holier-than-thou on me, Hunter. I caught you thinking about a new project this morning. Who never takes a vacation?"

"Okay, so you've got me there. But I'm not having sons. Even for Jack."

"Like I said—Peter Pan," Valerie said, tossing her long blond hair over her shoulder.

"And knock off the Peter Pan cracks, too."

"You know, Hunter, one of these days Daphne is going to get tired of taking care of you. She's going to find some nice doctor and—"

"Incorporate, I know."

"You should have talked to Noelle this morning. Now it's going to be awkward."

"No, it won't. I'll pretend nothing happened. It will give her an out. Maybe she won't even remember. She'd had a lot of champagne to drink at the rehearsal dinner."

"She'll remember."

"How do you know?"

"I'm a woman."

"No, you're not. You're a comic-book character. I created you. You think what I tell you to think."

"Right."

"Valerie—"

"Here comes Jack. Better not let him know you talk to yourself. He might have second thoughts about you fathering his grandsons." Valerie disappeared behind a tree.

"Look at all the balls I found, son," Jack said, emptying his bulging white shorts pockets. "Evidently I'm not the only one with a bad slice at this tee."

"I've been thinking, Jack...."

"What is it, son?"

"Well, I was wondering— How did you know when you were ready to have Sophie and Noelle? Did you just wake up one day and want babies, or what?"

Jack chortled. "I woke up one day and Grace told me she was pregnant. That's how I knew."

"Oh."

"Never regretted it for a moment. Let me tell you a secret about marriage, son. When it's bad, nothing's worse. Got a cousin who married the wrong woman. And that's a real sorry mess. But when it's right, you're over the moon. Grace and I got lucky. We were young and stupid kids and there have been times when we haven't had a dime. But we've always had each other. Always. And you can't touch that."

"You do seem to be a happy man."

"I only wish for Sophie and Marky the kind of happiness Grace and I have had. Though I have my reservations about the groom. I wish the same thing for you and Noelle."

Hunter didn't have the heart to tell him he was wishing down an empty well. "How about Freddie

Barton? I hear he was a pretty strong contender for Noelle's hand back a ways.''

Jack scowled. ''That peckerwood! He nearly broke my Noelle's heart back in high school. He was only interested in my money and disappeared fast when I lost it. He's cut out of the same cloth as Marky, I'm afraid. Just hope to heaven I'm wrong about that boy.''

Hunter nodded, not attempting any rebuttal. He held Marky in the same low esteem.

But it was none of his business.

If Sophie loved him, so be it. He'd put on his rented tuxedo and be the best man at the wedding.

Noelle hadn't heard Hunter leave to go play golf with her father. She wasn't aware that he wasn't still sleeping—far across the bed—until Sophie came in the room and began jumping up and down on the mattress insisting she get her lazy bones out of bed because they had dozens of things to do and Mother had a headache from obsessing over how much food to order for the reception since she was sure lots of guests were going to show up, even though they hadn't R.S.V.P.'d.

Sophie and Grace had already been to the photographer's to change the time for the shooting of bridal pictures. The next stop was the bakery where the final decision on the cake had to be made. Sophie insisted on having the cake gaudy with handmade sugar-dough flowers, each of which was priced separately—a fact that Noelle pointed out to her sister and her sister blatantly ignored.

Grace popped two more headache pills and agreed. Next, the florist's.

Noelle didn't take it as a good sign that the name of the florist's was Surprise! But everything went smoothly. For once, the three of them agreed on a simple wildflower arrangement that complemented the filmy pale pink dresses of the bridesmaids. The bridal bouquet was to be white roses and pink lilies.

The ordeal of the last-minute details out of the way, Grace insisted on going home to lie down. Although Noelle and Sophie had been planning to go out for lunch, they, too, opted to nap after first raiding the refrigerator.

"Sophie, why didn't you run away and elope?" Noelle asked, busily slicing fresh tomatoes for their BLT sandwiches. "Mom and Dad are going to go bankrupt paying for this wedding. All this planning for one day is a nightmare. No wonder mother has a headache. I'd never willingly go through all this. I can't believe you are. You're the one who started a picket march outside the third grade when they wouldn't let the girls go on the jungle gym. When did you go and get so traditional?"

Sophie shrugged, knifing some mayo out of a jar she took from the fridge. She spread the mayo on the slice of whole-wheat bread in her hand readying it for the bacon sizzling in the microwave.

"It's not my idea, I promise you."

"You mean it was Mother and Father's?"

"The big wedding is Marky's idea."

"*It is?*"

"He says the bigger the wedding, the more gifts—hopefully cash gifts. He wants to start his own business."

Noelle couldn't think of anything worse.

"What kind of business?" she asked, taking the bacon from the microwave when the ring signaled it was done.

"Promise you won't tell Father?"

"What is it?" Noelle asked, trying not to show her concern.

"Marky wants to start his own band. And I can be the singer."

Noelle bit her tongue to keep from saying what was on the tip of it. It would have made her sound too much as if she was Sophie's mother.

She'd always felt like Sophie's mother because of the ten-year age difference between them. When they were growing up she'd dressed Sophie up and played with her as though she was a baby doll. When Noelle was in high school, Sophie had tagged along wherever she could nag her sister into taking her. And when she couldn't—like when Noelle went out on dates—Sophie would sit on her bed and watch her big sister do her hair and makeup.

They hadn't shared boy stuff as they would have if they'd been closer in age, but they did have a bond that Noelle went out of her way to maintain. Sometimes that included keeping her mouth shut. She knew from memory that eighteen-year-olds didn't like advice, didn't listen to it and certainly didn't take it. No sense in wasting her breath and ruining their relationship.

"A band?"

"I know it sounds like a harebrained idea, Noelle. But it isn't, really. Marky is good. He's talented and all he needs is a chance. Don't you think it would be fun to sing with a band, didn't you ever want to do anything fun like that?"

Last night with Hunter flashed in her mind. "Sure. I've even done some kinda crazy things. But they don't always turn out the way you expect."

"I know that. But you have to try—or you'll never know."

There was something Noelle felt compelled to ask. Yes, she knew it was meddling. Yes, she knew Sophie was going to be annoyed. But she had to ask it, anyway.

"Sophie, we're sisters, right? You'd tell me if there was something wrong, wouldn't you?"

"What makes you think there's something wrong?" Sophie asked defensively, piling bacon high on her sandwich.

"I don't know. It's just this feeling I've got. You would tell me, wouldn't you?" She took a bite of her sandwich and chewed. "I mean, if there were something wrong..."

"Noelle..."

"Okay, okay."

"There's nothing wrong."

"Marky?"

"Yeah," Marky said belligerently. He leaned against the kitchen wall in the Perrys' home, cupping the receiver tightly as he listened.

"Did you tell her?" a female voice badgered him.

"The time hasn't been right," he said defensively.

"There isn't any more time. Tell her now," she ordered.

"I said I'd tell her," he whined.

"See that you do." Once again, Marky heard the now familiar slam of a phone receiver.

When Marky hung up the wall phone in the kitchen, Hunter turned and went to the stairs. He'd planned on getting a drink from the refrigerator when Marky's furtive, tense conversation had stopped him. He'd lingered just outside the door to eavesdrop.

The time wasn't right for what? Hunter wondered. Who was Marky supposed to tell what?

Hunter shook his head and banished his questions.

It was none of his business.

Still, the tone of Marky's voice bothered him. He'd seemed both scared and out of control.

Noelle took Hunter's lead and pretended nothing had happened between them. Perhaps he assumed that since she'd drunk so much champagne at the rehearsal dinner, she wouldn't remember.

She did.

All too well.

It had been heady pleasure. A rush. A sensual feast. Right up until the moment Hunter had ruined it.

Really, it wasn't his fault. After all, he'd only pointed out the truth. It was she who was at fault for forgetting he was only her bought and paid-for date.

It wasn't a mistake she'd make again. But now that she had a grip on how he saw things, she'd take what he offered and not build up false hopes.

She glanced over at him as he drove to the next shopping mall on the list. They'd spent over an hour combing the mall for a dress for her and a tuxedo for him. Finally they'd stumbled across a rental shop where Hunter found a tux—and he looked drop-dead handsome in it.

If she'd gone to the doctor with a case of the blahs, he'd be just the tonic the doctor would have ordered. What more could a woman need to instantly lift her spirits than a blond, blue-eyed charmer?

And rich to boot. Once Sophie had pointed out how famous Hunter was, she realized she'd misjudged him.

As they reached the Frontenac mall Noelle hoped that she would find something to wear to the wedding here and not have to spend the day hitting every single shopping center in St. Louis.

"Father was in a good mood," Noelle said, as Hunter parked her father's car and they walked toward the mall. "I guess you took my advice and let him win the golf game this morning. Or did he find a cache of golf balls in the woods?"

"Both."

"Let's try this shop first. They usually have something I like," Noelle suggested when they came to one of the more popular chain boutiques in the mall.

"No."

Noelle turned and looked at Hunter.

"No?"

"I've called ahead and made an appointment for us at Concepts."

"You did what?"

"My treat," he said, smiling expansively.

"Why?"

"So you let me pick out the outfit."

"Hunter, did anyone ever tell you you give good bribes?" Concepts was an exclusive designer shop she'd never even gone in because the air was too rare-fied to breathe.

"And I need a favor from you," he added.

"What kind of favor?" she demanded suspiciously.

"I need you to help me pick something out before we leave. I see Concepts, it's over there." He held the big glass door open for her, then followed her in.

She felt like a sacrificial lamb as the saleslady with lacquered hair and nails approached her. The woman openly disapproved of Noelle's off-the-rack ribbed top and pleated shorts.

"May I help you?" the saleslady asked, her tone clearly conveying that Noelle was in the wrong store.

Just as Noelle was about to say something biting to the snotty salesclerk Hunter came up behind her.

"We have an appointment. I'm Hunter Ashton."

In a snap, the saleslady's attitude shifted from snotty to fawning. "Yes, Mr. Hunter. We have a room for you," the woman said, turning to lead the way.

"A room?" Noelle mouthed, glancing back over her shoulder at Hunter.

The dressing room had faux marble walls and thick beige carpeting. Hunter sat in the wing chair to the left of the wall mirror.

"What would you like to see?" the saleslady asked.

"We need a dress and a pair of shoes," Hunter informed her.

The saleslady glanced over at Noelle and then back at Hunter. "Size ten?"

"Yes, a ten," he answered a little too smugly, a little too possessively, Noelle thought. She felt like a harem girl.

"And will this be a formal occasion, sir?"

"Yes, it's a wedding reception."

The woman nodded. "Nothing white."

Noelle wasn't used to being part of the furniture. She didn't even let a date order for her at dinner, for heaven's sake. She was about to speak up when Hunter said, "Red, I think. We'll see whatever you have in red."

"Red."

Hunter nodded. "The sexier the better."

The saleslady glanced back over at Noelle, said nothing, then went to find something red, the sexier the better.

Noelle gave Hunter a look of censure.

"Isn't this fun?" he responded, refusing to be put down.

Noelle crossed her arms in front of her chest. "You do this a lot?"

Hunter shook his head no. "First time. But I kinda like it. I feel sorta like a—"

The door to the dressing room opened and the saleslady brought in two red dresses and held them up. One was a slinky flared-skirted dress with a sweetheart neckline.

Hunter shook his head no.

"Leave the other one," he told her, nodding at the red stretch-lace slip dress in an-above-the-knee length.

The saleslady did as he instructed.

Noelle continued to stand with her arms crossed in front of her, as she eyed the skimpy dress.

"It won't bite. Come on, be a sport and at least try it on, Noelle."

She'd have to take everything off to try on the dress and he knew it. And was enjoying it.

She uncrossed her arms and lifted the hanger from the hook where the saleslady had hung the dress. She held the provocative red garment against her body and looked at her reflection in the mirror. It wasn't a dress she herself would ever have imagined trying on, much less buying, much less wearing.

But she'd promised herself a weekend adventure. Now was not the time to chicken out—not completely, anyway.

She looked over at Hunter who was sprawled in the chair, lazily watching her. Daring her.

"And what will you be doing while I'm trying this on?" she asked him pointedly. It wasn't pitch-dark in the dressing room the way it had been in her room last night. The lights here were spotlight bright.

Hunter pushed himself up from the chair reluctantly and stood. "I'll see what's holding up the shoes I asked to see." Making good on his promise, he left the dressing room in search of them, closing the door behind him.

Noelle laid the dress on the chair Hunter had vacated, and quickly began slipping out of her clothes, planning to be in the red dress before he returned. Her shorts, top and front-clasp bra landed on the floor in a heap. When she fiddled with the spaghetti strap that got hung up on the hanger, a few choice nonconservative-banker phrases erupted.

Freeing it at last, she scrunched the dress in her hands and pulled it over her body. Oh, my. It looked like lingerie. Very expensive lingerie, mind you. There was nothing subtle about the dress. She kicked off her sandals. Better. Could she really wear a dress like this?

"Well, what do you think?" Hunter asked, coming back into the dressing room.

"It's red," she answered his reflection in the mirror.

His reflection held up a pair of red satin high heels with ankle-wrap ribbon ties.

"Oh, my," she said aloud, swallowing dryly.

"Come sit down and I'll put them on for you. They're perfect for this dress. You are going to look so hot. It's a good thing ol' Freddie Barton won't be at the wedding. He'd go home and hang himself."

Noelle smiled at his compliment and took a seat.

"How did you know the size?" she asked, when the one he slipped on fit her. "Do you have a foot fetish?"

"I overheard Sophie and your mother discussing storing her wedding dress and stuff for you in case you wanted it some day when you got married. They decided against the shoes because she wears a five and you wear two sizes bigger. Do these wraps tie in front or in back?''

''In front, in bows.''

''Good, it's easier that way.'' Several attempts later Hunter had both shoes on her and tied in saucy bows. ''Okay, let's have a look.'' He stood and moved back so she could go to the mirror.

Noelle rose and took a few cautious steps, making sure she could walk at all in the precarious spike heels. Confident that she could navigate without pitching forward, she moved to study her reflection in the mirror.

''I don't know, Hunter,'' she said, looking in the mirror at her image.

''You don't like it?'' A note of disappointment tinged his voice.

''It's not that, exactly.'' In truth, she found it all rather exciting. The dress was indeed starting to grow on her. In fact, it made her feel pretty sexy. ''Don't you think, though, that it's a little...''

''Hot? Yeah!''

''I don't know....'' She tugged at the dress where it clung to her hips.

''Wait a minute. I know what's wrong.'' Hunter moved to stand behind her, inching his fingertips beneath the stretchy red lace material.

''Hunter, what are you—''

''Your panties ruin the line of the dress,'' he answered, inching them down.

''Hunter!''

"See, look," he said, when he'd accomplished his mission.

He was right, she saw, stepping out of her panties and studying her reflection. *If* she wore the dress, she'd have to wear it with panty house and nothing else.

"What do you think?" he asked, coaxing.

"I bet it cost a small fortune. I can't let you..." she began hedging.

"Let me, please—"

"Don't you think you're going a little overboard trying to give me what I paid for?" she couldn't resist saying. It was so easy to get caught up in the fantasy that he was nothing more than a regular date. But regular dates didn't look like him—at least hers hadn't. And they didn't buy you designer dresses that looked like expensive lingerie. Her whole family would be shocked if she showed up in it.

"I deserve that," Hunter said. "But only because you took it the wrong way."

"How was I supposed to take it?"

"It wasn't what I meant. It came out all wrong. I'm the one who got lucky in this deal, Noelle."

He was a smooth talker. Real smooth.

"Let me buy you the dress to make up, please. I'll feel better."

She looked in the mirror at the dress one last time.

"You really think it looks okay?" Was she making a mistake? Oh, hell, what was the point of having an adventure if you played it safe?

"Let's take it."

"Right decision," Hunter agreed, pulling her into his arms to celebrate it with a kiss. His fingers tightened at her back as the kiss surged to an unsettling depth, taking her by surprise.

Noelle had to admit that Hunter was a special man. The kind of man who could make her the kind of woman no man before him had been able to. He sensed the part of her she kept hidden—even from herself.

He was coaxing every facet of her to come out and play with him. To come into the light from the shadows of repression.

He was the kind of man who wanted her to ask for what she wanted and to take pleasure in it.

The room was small.

The dress was hot.

The next thing she knew, the dress was off, tossed at the hanger in their haste.

Hunter walked her backward to the chair and settled her in it, kissing her senseless all the while. He moved back from her and rested on his knees. "Lordy, these shoes, Miss Noellie..." Hunter said, kissing her instep with baby kisses that tickled deliciously, that teased and promised to inch toward her ankle.

Noelle laughed, taking pleasure in the teasing...in Hunter's playful seduction. The shoes were indeed a piece of work. They had very little to do with walking, even less to do with comfort.

Feeling reckless and emboldened, she decided to try to beat Hunter at his own game. "Give me a clue, Hunter. Where do you want these fanciful, sinfully impractical shoes—around your neck or mine?"

"I thought you'd never ask, but since you have—" His grin was wicked as he lifted her knees and settled the red satin shoes around his shoulders.

"I was kidding!" Noelle squealed as he began kissing his way up her calf to her inner thigh in earnest, nipping and licking and growling.

"Hunter!" she cried out when he moved dangerously high on her inner thigh with his titillating kisses, his hand stroking lightly.

"Shush, woman," Hunter whispered. "Do you want to bring store security?"

"Oh, Hunter, you did lock the dressing-room door, didn't you?" Noelle reminded.

"Lock the door?" Hunter echoed, looking up at Noelle.

"But I thought you knew, it doesn't lock," he said on a quick breath, then had her screaming his name again.

"Hunter! Ah...ahhh...*Hunter!*"

6

"So Hunter, what did Noelle pick out for me?" Valerie asked, adjusting her red bustier.

"Go away, there are no girls allowed at a bachelor party."

"You forgot, didn't you?"

"Don't worry, I promised you a new outfit and you'll get it on the next project."

"I'm not wearing those red shoes, Hunter. You can forget it." Valerie stood in the doorway with her arms crossed.

Hunter flushed and returned to the poker table. He was down a hundred, but then his mind wasn't on the cards. Noelle was playing havoc with his concentration—no matter what he was doing.

"I hear you're replacing me as best man," Freddie said, tossing in his cards. He wasn't playing much better than Hunter.

"Rented the tuxedo today. How's your leg feeling?"

"Damn thing is uncomfortable as hell." He patted the leg in the cast propped up on a folding chair. "Doc says I have to have this cast on for six-to-eight weeks. I'm not looking forward to it, I'll tell you."

"You weren't looking backward, either, when you fell off the dock," Marky said to a chorus of laughter.

"You're fired, Marky."

"Again? Don't you think you should wait till you're out of the cast? Right now you need me to bring you coffee and drive you home."

"Okay, you're fired in six-to-eight weeks," Freddie grumbled without meaning it.

Hunter glanced at the fluorescent-orange lightweight cast on Freddie's leg. "That's some cast you've got there, Freddie. I hate to tell you, but it's going to clash with Noelle's dress, so don't stand by her, okay? The dress is really sexy. Too bad you won't be able to dance with her."

Freddie mumbled something else that he did mean.

"Pizza's here!" one of Marky's friends called out from the door.

Hunter groaned. Pizza, his ass.

He'd bet the pot it was a stripper. He was getting too old for this. That thought pulled him up short. Hell, he was only twenty-eight. Since when was he not interested in a woman taking off her clothes?

Daphne would be glad to know that maybe Peter Pan was growing up. That just maybe he'd found a grown-up woman, too.

Noelle was home alone.

Hunter and her father were at the bachelor party for Marky.

Sophie was at her own bachelorette party, which Noelle had begged off because of a headache.

And her mother had gone out for dinner with some friends.

Noelle went downstairs to rummage in the refrigerator for something to nibble on. Not feeling very inspired, she wound up settling for a toasted cheese sandwich and a cold glass of milk. She sat down and stared at the food. The whole evening she'd been unable to concentrate on anything. Anything but Hunter.

What had started out as a straightforward arrangement was getting increasingly complicated. Reading Hunter was difficult. Just when she had pegged him as a devil-may-care wastrel, he'd turned out to be rich and famous. That meant he was capable of discipline, that he was a responsible person.

But he sure did like to play—and he was good at it. Maybe she herself had gone overboard on leaving play out of her life. Work, while satisfying, was not a whole life.

Her problem was twofold when it came to Hunter.

One, was Hunter just having a good time, an adventure, with her? Was she reading more into what was happening than was really there? And two, if she wasn't, could she have a relationship with a man like Hunter? Could she adjust to his spontaneous, live-for-the-moment style of living? She hadn't much success at it as a child.

Still, it could be done. Her parents and Sophie seemed to thrive on it. Turmoil didn't seem to distress them the way it distressed her. In fact they flourished in that kind of chaos.

Even now, when she suspected her parents were flirting with bankruptcy again and Sophie was entering into a questionable marriage, she was the only one who was worried.

Sophie.

Only her sister would marry a boy because she wanted to sing in the band. Even at eighteen, Noelle hadn't been that young. At eighteen she'd been more concerned with her SATs than boys, and marriage had been the furthest thing from her mind.

But it was more than just the foolishness of her eighteen-year-old sister's decision making that bothered Noelle. There was something wrong. Something Sophie either didn't know, or wasn't telling her.

Had Sophie changed her mind but didn't have the guts to cancel at such a late hour? Maybe she didn't have the nerve to disappoint their parents—Noelle smiled—and leave her mother with "all that potato salad" she seemed so obsessed over.

At the bottom of everything was Sophie's wedding's effect on *her.* It was forcing her to think about marriage. Did she ever plan to marry? Why? Or why not?

It was a subject that she hadn't had the time or energy to give much thought to while climbing the corporate banking ladder. But she needed a personal life, too. And Hunter had shown her she desperately needed some fun in her life. She didn't need to worry about everything so much. Control was an illusion anyway, if you thought it through. Anything could and usually did happen over the course of a life, and it usually wasn't what you expected. It was time she took some risks.

And any way you looked at it—Hunter was a risk.

Noelle wiped up her crumbs and put her dish and glass in the sink. Tomorrow was a busy day, so she might as well go to bed early and get as much sleep as possible.

She saw Sophie had left the light on in her room when she left.

As she walked down the hall to her sister's room, she smiled, recalling another room—the dressing room at Concepts. It all seemed like some incredible dream. Had Hunter really taken her there? Had he really bought her that sexy red dress and shoes? Would she really have the nerve to wear them?

Nerve. She'd nearly lost it when Hunter had told her the dressing-room door didn't lock! Only later did he explain that he'd paid the saleslady to give them some time alone.

The thrill of danger had only been in her imagination. The look of censure on the saleslady's face as they left, however, had been real.

The woman needed to get a life, Noelle thought, and then laughed. Good advice that she herself should take.

When she reached to turn off the light in Sophie's room, her gaze was caught by another spectacular dress—a white one.

Sophie's wedding dress.

It was the first time she'd seen it. She crossed the room to where the dress hung on a door hook.

The dress suited an eighteen-year-old. It had Fairy Princess written all over it. White, beaded Alençon lace made up the fitted bodice. The neckline was off-the-shoulder tulle and the full skirt was a puff of tulle.

At the sight of it even a twenty-eight-year-old melted, despite her best defenses. Noelle reached out and touched the magical wedding dress.

On impulse, she lifted the hanger off the hook and went to the mirror on the wall, holding the dress up in front of her. She swayed as if she were dancing.

Caught up, she acted out of character and slipped the frothy dress from the padded hanger.

Dare she? she wondered, pausing. No one would know if she tried it on. She was four inches taller than Sophie, but the dress would fit otherwise, because she and her sister both wore the same size.

It was amazing what you could talk yourself into when you were alone and no one would know. Quickly, she slipped out of her clothes, shedding them in a pile on the floor. She stepped into the dress and gingerly zipped the long zipper up the back.

On her the dress was ankle-length instead of floor-length, but the image reflecting back at her was appealing. It occurred to her that she had tried on several new images since being with Hunter.

She wondered what Hunter would think if he could see her in the bridal gown? Did he ever think of marriage? Probably not. As a celebrity, he probably had women swooning over him all the time. Men seldom worried about balancing a career and a marriage. Seldom had to. It was women's work.

But if two people worked on it maybe they could create a marriage that would suit both of them as if it were tailor-made. She really was daydreaming. There probably couldn't be a worse candidate for marriage than someone like Hunter, who spent most of his time in the fantasy world of comics—a place where women saved the world wearing red bustiers and thigh-high suede boots.

A noise in the house startled her. Thinking quickly and identifying where exactly the noise had come from, she froze when she realized it was at the top of the stairs.

Someone had come home early!

It didn't matter who. Being caught in Sophie's wedding dress would be mortifying.

She had to get out of the dress fast.

But she couldn't move. The footsteps were already coming down the hall toward Sophie's bedroom. There wasn't time—and no way could she hide in the frothy confection.

Wait, Hunter wouldn't come to Sophie's room, she reasoned on a sigh of relief. That meant it was Sophie. Somehow she'd have to explain— No, wait. She heard footsteps, plural. It had to be her parents. But why would they...?

She turned to the open door and took a deep breath, trying not to let her nervousness show. It was no use. She felt like a little girl caught playing with her mother's makeup. She felt ridiculous.

But it wasn't her parents.

Fear replaced embarrassment when she saw the two big guys filling the doorway to Sophie's room.

"We want to talk to you, Sophie," the taller one said.

"I'm not—" she started to say, then clamped her lips shut.

"Come on. Don't give us any trouble, okay? Let's get out of here before someone comes home and someone winds up getting hurt," the younger one said, looking around to check the hall.

"Go?" Noelle backed away from them, trying to make herself a smaller target. In the bridal gown, she felt like a huge spider.

"Don't be alarmed. We're not going to hurt you. We're just going for a little ride. All we want to do is talk to you."

Don't be alarmed? He had to be kidding. She was shaking, she was so scared. Two strange men wanted her to go for a little ride and she shouldn't be alarmed? What if they were nut cases? She checked and didn't see a gun. That relieved her somewhat, but the two guys were still awfully big.

"What do you want?" she demanded, trying to sound a lot braver than she felt.

"We'll tell you what we want in the car. Quit stalling and come outside with us. If you cooperate, you'll see that everything will be fine."

"If you try to make me leave with you, I'll scream," she threatened.

"No, you won't," they assured her.

"Then at least let me change out of this," Noelle said, playing for time, praying for Hunter to show up early, after all. "If I leave this house in my wedding dress, I'll look ridiculous...and suspicious."

"It doesn't matter what you're wearing. No one is going to see you because it's dark outside. Listen to me. There isn't time to change. This has to be done quickly. Come with us and don't cause a scene," the younger man coaxed.

"Where are we going?"

They didn't answer her. The two looked enough alike to be brothers. And they seemed nervous, like this wasn't something they did all the time. Noelle didn't know whether to be relieved or worried about that.

"I'm not going anywhere with you," she said, finally trying to bluff her way out of whatever situation her sister had gotten herself into.

"We're leaving *now*. Shut up and do as we say or we'll have to..." The older guy started advancing toward her, forcing her bluff.

"What?" Noelle demanded.

"Escort you out," they chorused. The younger guy also approached and they did just that, each of them taking her arm and hustling her out of the room and into the hall.

"Let me go," Noelle cried, trying to pull free of their grip. The two men held her firmly and lifted her off her feet to get her down the stairs.

For one brief hysterical moment all she could think about was that there was going to be a headline on the cover of one of those awful tabloids and her captioned picture in Sophie's wedding dress. Her career in banking would be over.

It took some doing but they got her in the car. She found herself in the back seat of a seventies Chevy. It was one of those boat-size models so she, the dress and the younger guy fit. The bigger guy drove.

"Why are you doing this? Where are we going? What's going on?" Noelle was full of questions they were unwilling to answer.

All the driver said was, "You'll find out soon enough. You don't have to worry about us, we mean you no harm. There's just something that you have to know before you marry Marky."

The guys seemed sincere about no harm coming to her. And as they hadn't been brandishing a weapon or been menacing, she took a deep breath and tried to keep her anxiety down.

What was Sophie's prospective groom involved in? It could be anything from gambling to bank robbing. Oh, no, she hoped that wasn't what this was all about. Had Freddie mentioned to Marky that she was vice president of a bank? It came back to her that Marky worked as a mechanic for Freddie Barton in his car dealership.

A chop shop, she thought all at once. Maybe that was it. Maybe Freddie was involved up to his fluorescent-orange cast. Maybe that was why Freddie had a broken leg to begin with.

She tried to straighten the bridal gown in case she got out of this somehow and could return the dress to its hanger without evidence of it having been worn.

"How do the two of you know Marky?" she asked, attempting to make conversation.

"We don't know Marky," they informed her in unison.

"You've never heard his band...?" she prompted, searching for some connection.

"I heard his band was pretty good," the younger guy beside her said. "But I've never heard it myself. Have you, brother Ben?" Brother Ben didn't comment, just looked straight ahead.

Brother Ben. Did that mean they were brothers, or were they in some sort of religious cult? Did they want Marky to belong to the cult? Did Marky already belong to the cult? Was there even a cult? Her headache was even worse than it had been before.

This was definitely not her idea of a good adventure.

"So, are the two of you brothers?"

"Yeah," the guy in front said curtly. He'd seemed to be waiting for some signal to put the car in gear and drive away. Whatever it was, he got it. They started rolling.

"Why don't you just tell me what I need to know? Why do we have to go somewhere? Can't you tell me here and let me go back inside before someone sees me in this?"

At the end of the block the driver pulled the car over alongside a woman and stopped. What was this—a serial kidnapping?

When the young woman opened the car door to get in, Noelle could see she was about seven months pregnant. This was some strange gang that was kidnapping her.

"Did you tell her?" the woman asked the driver, once she'd closed the door and they were driving away.

"No, I thought you wanted to tell her."

"Oh, great. You've probably scared her half to death, Ben."

"Yeah, he has," Noelle piped in from the back seat.

The woman turned around and stared at Noelle in complete surprise. "Who are you?"

"What do you mean, who is she?" the guy beside Noelle retorted. "She's Marky's intended."

"No, she's not."

"Of course, she is," Ben said. "She's wearing the wedding dress, isn't she? Who else but the bride would be trying on her wedding dress the night before the wedding?"

"You tell me, Ben. I've seen Sophie and that ain't her."

Now all three of them were staring at Noelle, Ben in the rearview mirror as he drove.

"I'm not Sophie," Noelle said, stating the obvious.

"Then why are you wearing her wedding dress?" Ben asked.

"I don't have a good answer for that one," Noelle replied. "It was a dumb impulse, okay?"

"But *who* are you?" the woman demanded.

"I'm Sophie's sister, Noelle."

"Now what?" Ben demanded. "Do you want me to keep driving or should we take her back?"

"What are you planning to do, exchange her for Sophie? Don't be an idiot. Just drive, okay? Let me think. I can't believe I have brothers who can't even carry out a simple—"

"It was an easy mistake—she's in the wedding gown," the guy beside Noelle said defensively. "They're sisters, so they look alike. How were we to know?"

"Just be quiet and let me think," his sister said. People kept waving when they saw a bride in the back seat. Every time they stopped at a light Noelle hid her face. All she needed was for someone to recognize her.

Now that she knew the situation wasn't really threatening, she wanted to know what was going on.

"Why don't we just tell her?" Ben finally suggested.

"Yeah, she can tell Sophie."

"There doesn't seem to be any choice since you guys screwed everything up."

The woman turned around to look at Noelle. "I'm Polly Palmer."

"And she's pregnant," Ben added, accusingly.

"I'm sure she's noticed, Ben."

"Tell her who the father is," Ben urged.

"I'm getting to it, okay?" She looked Noelle straight in the eye and said what Noelle had the sinking feeling was coming. "Your sister, Sophie, is marrying my baby's father in the morning."

Noelle didn't know what to say.

So she didn't say anything. She was too stunned. How was she going to tell Sophie? *Should* she tell Sophie? And if she did, would Sophie blame her? Would Sophie ever forgive Noelle for ruining her wedding? *Would* it ruin the wedding? Or would Sophie marry Marky anyway? How much in love with Marky was Sophie?

All those questions ran through Noelle's mind.

All those and one more.

Was this woman telling the truth?

She had to ask. But how to put it?

"How—ah—I mean, are you sure the baby is Marky's?" she finally said.

"I'm sure. There isn't anyone else but Marky. I love him. And I know he loves me."

"So then why is he marrying my sister?"

"Because he's afraid."

"I don't understand," Noelle said, puzzled. Marky was afraid of Sophie? Sophie was about as threatening as a butterfly.

"Hey, here's a Taco Bell. Can we stop? I'm hungry," the brother seated beside Noelle said, pointing to the Mexican restaurant on the corner.

"Sam, now is not the time to—"

"Get him something to eat, you know he's hypoglycemic. Pull in the drive-through lane," his sister said protectively. "I could go for a taco salad, myself."

Ben did as his sister ordered. Polly didn't seem shy about getting her way. So why was she in her situation? Noelle decided there was more to the story.

"You said Marky was afraid. What does that have to do with his marrying my sister?"

"Sophie wants to get married to Marky because she thinks if she's married to him, it guarantees she will be the singer for his band."

"Are you saying Sophie is marrying Marky to be in a band? That that's the only reason?"

"Yeah, and the only reason Marky is marrying Sophie is because he loves me. Marky needs her. He's afraid the record contract he has lined up will fall through without her as the singer. He's afraid if he tells Sophie he doesn't want to get married, she'll quit the band.''

"What a mess." Noelle buried her head in her hands, while Ben placed an order for their food into the squawky speaker. He looked at Noelle. "Do you want something to eat?''

"No. Listen, if I promise to tell Sophie, will you let me out here? I can't get taco sauce all over Sophie's wedding dress. She'll kill me.''

They let her out.

Once she was outside the car, she wondered about the wisdom of what she had just done. A woman in a wedding dress stood out like a sore thumb. And to top it off, she was barefoot. Sophie's shoes were too small, so she hadn't tried them on with the wedding dress.

But even worse, she didn't have a cent on her. No identification. Nothing.

She looked back to the Palmers' car, but they'd already gone through the pickup area and left with their food. There was only one thing for her to do. She would have to ask someone to lend her a quarter to call...who?

Only one name came to mind.

Hunter.

The night kept getting worse.

The trouble was there wasn't much foot traffic. Most people were in cars. And the few people she tried to borrow change from gave her a wide berth, thinking it was some kind of prank or setup.

Her head was pounding and her feet were dirty, but the wedding dress so far seemed to have held up, she noticed, as she waited at the stoplight, summoning the courage to go across the street to the bowling alley. It was going to take a lot of nerve to walk in there and beg for a quarter.

She looked like an abandoned bride.

This was definitely not turning out to be the sort of adventure she'd had in mind for the weekend.

When and if she got Sophie's dress back home safe and sound, she was never, ever, doing anything even remotely impulsive again. She simply didn't have the stomach or the nerves for it.

The light changed and she limped across the walkway, having stepped on a bit of gravel. When she crossed the bowling-alley parking lot she was careful not to brush the pristine white gown against any of the cars. When she got to the entrance of the bowling alley she paused to take a deep breath and calm her jittery nerves.

She had to think, to concentrate on one thing at a time. Otherwise, she'd be overwhelmed and do nothing.

First, the quarter for the phone call to Hunter. She closed her eyes and prayed he was still at Freddie Barton's. Freddie, of course, would have been the one to throw the bachelor party for Marky.

Steeling her resolve, she pushed open the heavy glass door to the bowling alley and went inside. She'd forgotten how noisy bowling alleys were. The crash of the balls into the pins and the camaraderie made up a steady din.

A middle-aged man stood at the desk renting bowling shoes. He had a kind face. Maybe he would lend her a quarter to make a phone call. Maybe he'd even let her do it without asking questions. She waited for the two teenage boys who were admiring an expensive bowling ball in the glass display case below the counter to leave, and then she walked up to the rental desk.

"Hello," he said with a straight face.

She nodded.

"Will that be a party of two bowling?" he asked, in a blasé tone. Not much seemed to surprise him, she thought.

"No. Ah, I'm not planning to bowl."

"I see."

"I've had, ah, I missed a connection and I was wondering if I could borrow a quarter to call for a ride?" She hoped she didn't faint—that was all she needed to make the evening complete. She willed herself to breathe evenly.

"There's no need to borrow a quarter, miss. I can dial the number for you, if you like," he offered, picking up the telephone on the desk.

"Um, do you have a phone book," she asked, feeling even more embarrassed.

"Sure, of course." He turned and lifted one from beneath the counter.

"Freddie...please be listed," she murmured beneath her breath, as she flipped through the pages till she came to the Bs and then to Barton...Frederick James.

It was listed!

She read the phone number off to the man and he dialed it for her.

She watched his face anxiously. "It's busy," he said, hanging up the phone.

She felt her shoulders slump in defeat.

"Tell you what, I noticed you've lost your shoes. Why don't you put these on so your feet don't get hurt, and I'll try the number again in a minute."

He handed her a pair of size-seven red-and-green bowling shoes.

How could she refuse when he was only being nice?

She accepted the shoes and sat down to put them on while the man took pity on her and bought her a soda.

"Let's try again," he said after handing her the drink. Noelle jumped up when the man smiled and said, "It's ringing."

She took the phone.

"Freddie? Is Hunter there? Could I talk to him, please?"

"Wait a minute, I think he was leaving a bit ago. Let me check."

Oh, please, she silently prayed.

"Noelle?"

It was Hunter!

"Yes, it's me, Hunter. I need to have you do me a favor. Would you mind terribly leaving the bachelor party and coming to pick me up at the Red Bird Bowling Alley? I'm sort of stranded here."

"Are you okay? You sound strange."

"I'm . . . I'm okay. Just pick me up. Right away."

"Where will you be waiting?"

"I'll be at the door. The bowling alley is at the corner of Hampton and Gravois. Don't worry, you won't miss me when you get here. I'll be the one in a wedding dress and bowling shoes."

7

Noelle finished her soda, thanked the nice man who'd got busy at the desk from a rush of customers, then went to wait by the door of the bowling alley to watch for Hunter. She endured a lot of curious glances and some outright stares as people came and went. It was a busy Friday date-night. If her mind hadn't been taken up with worry about what she was going to do about Polly Palmer's bombshell news, she'd have been truly mortified. As it was, she had more pressing problems than her strange attire.

Finally, after what seemed like hours, her knight in the white limo arrived. As he pulled up to the entrance, she stepped outside to meet him.

He parked the limo and got out.

She knew he was chewing the inside of his cheek to keep from laughing at the sight she must be. Still, he was unable to resist a wisecrack.

"Are you ready to go, or did you want to bowl a couple of games first?" he asked, eyeing her shoes.

She looked down at the shoes, then back up at him and glared.

"Guess not," Hunter said, opening the rear door of the limo to accommodate the bridal gown.

Noelle piled in, taking care every layer of the tulle skirt cleared the door before he closed it.

While Hunter walked around to his side of the car, she hastily removed the ugly bowling shoes and shoved them at him when he opened the driver's door. "Would you run these back inside for me and give the guy a dollar?"

Hunter took the shoes and did as she asked without giving her any further trouble.

While he was inside she tried to think of something plausible to tell him to explain why she was dressed as she was.

When Hunter returned to the car he glanced back at her. "Where to?"

"Home, and quickly."

"Are you running away from a groom? And more important, is he armed?"

"There is no groom," she answered through clenched teeth. "This is Sophie's wedding dress."

"I see."

Clearly, he didn't.

"Just drive and I'll explain it to you on the way, okay?"

Hunter put the limo in motion while Noelle cast about for a way to begin. "Did you ever do something impulsive when you were alone and thought no one would ever know?"

"You mean like smear your body with tuna fish and let the cat lick it off?"

She glanced up in the rearview mirror and saw that he was joking.

"I mean, like try on a wedding dress...."

"Oh."

She waited, knowing he wouldn't let it drop at that. This was too good.

"Trying on the wedding dress, that's not so bad— we all give in to the occasional bad urge. Going to the bowling alley in it and renting shoes is kinda where you lose me. There seems to be some sort of gap there, when—"

"I didn't plan to.... Going to a bowling alley, going anywhere in Sophie's dress wasn't—" She gave up in frustration. "Just take me home."

"Do you think that's wise?"

"Where exactly do you think I should be going? I've got to get this dress home."

She saw Hunter glance at the dash.

"It's ten o'clock. I'm sure your parents are on their way home from dinner by now. You don't want them to—"

"No, of course not. But I don't know what else to do."

The night just kept getting worse. She started to cry.

"Oh, now, don't start doing that. Listen, I've got an idea. Why don't we find you something else to wear? Then I can drop you off at the bachelorette party so you can stall Sophie on the off chance the party was to break up early. While you're doing that, I'll find a way to sneak in the wedding dress."

"You'd do that for me?" she sniffed.

"Of course. I aim to please."

Right, part of the thousand-dollar bargain, Noelle thought glumly.

"Where am I going to find something to change into? The malls are all already closed."

"Let me think. We could try the supermarket, but all we'd find there are T-shirts and I don't think you want to go bar-hopping in just a T-shirt." He turned and checked just to be sure.

"I'd rather wear the wedding dress."

"Okay, okay. I know—we'll cruise the laundromats until we find someone who's left their clothes to dry."

"We can't do that!"

"Do you want to get the dress back home without anyone knowing, or not?"

"I guess...."

It took them a half hour, but they finally found a laundromat with the dryers circling and no one around. Hunter parked the limo and while Noelle played lookout leaning over the front seat by the horn, he went inside the laundromat and lifted some clothing for her.

He came back with it stuffed beneath his polo shirt, got in the car and tossed it back to her.

"These are guy's clothes," she complained, as Hunter pulled away.

"Beggars can't be choosers. I'll loan you my belt if the jeans don't fit."

She struggled out of the wedding dress, a task made easier by its off-the-shoulder style. She didn't need Hunter's belt. The jeans fit, if she didn't plan to breathe. She pulled on the dark tank top and tried to imagine the guy's clothes she was wearing as comfortable. In truth, she was as uncomfortable in a strange man's clothes as she'd been in the wedding dress. But she didn't say anything because Hunter was doing the best he could to help.

"Are you dressed?" Hunter asked from the front seat, slamming on the brakes as someone ran a red light.

"Yes, I'm dressed."

"Okay, then, we're off to find Sophie. Any ideas?"

Noelle thought for a moment. "I know. We can find her by the bus. They rented a bus to go bar-hopping since they would all be drinking. And they were going down to the Landing. We'll just cruise until we find the bus."

They took the bumpy ride down the cobblestone streets of Laclede's Landing, but there wasn't a parked bus to be seen.

"Maybe it did break up early," Noelle said with a sigh of resignation. "Wait—let's try Soulard. They might have gone to one of the bars there."

Ten minutes later they sighted the bus outside the most outrageously funky establishment in Soulard— one with a wildly colorful decorated hearse parked outside. Hunter let Noelle out so she could make sure Sophie's group was inside the Venice Café. In minutes she was waving him on from the doorway.

Taking his cue, Hunter drove away with the wedding dress in the back of the limo before anyone came outside and saw it.

He turned on the radio and hit Highway 55 as the quickest route back. It was a golden oldies station, and an old Motown hit of the Temptations came on. He was singing and grinning, still recalling how Noelle had looked in the wedding dress and bowling shoes. His blond creation appeared on the seat beside him.

"Don't start liking those bowling shoes too much, Hunter," Valerie said. "I'm not saving the world in bowling shoes, either. And I'm getting impatient to know what my new outfit is going to be."

"I guess you want combat boots, right?"

"Yeah, that'd be cool. It's what Madonna wore on Letterman. I could handle that." Valerie looked in the rearview mirror, applying blood-red lipstick.

"Well, I couldn't. Forget the combat boots," Hunter said, turning up the radio to drown out Valerie's pestering.

"How about some nice, tall, shiny black boots that come up to my knees?"

"Where'd you get that idea?"

"Must be the siren that made me think of them. You know, they're the kind state troopers wear."

Hunter heard it then and saw the flashing red lights. With a sinking feeling in the pit of his stomach, he knew he was the one being pulled over for speeding.

He slowed and followed the beam of light from the trooper's flashlight directing him to the shoulder of the highway behind a red sports car that had also gotten caught.

He waited impatiently as the trooper dealt with the guy in the sports car, making the driver take the breathalizer test. Hunter tried to recall how long it had been since he'd had a beer at the bachelor party.

He wasn't a heavy drinker, but he could have beer on his breath. All he needed was to be taken in and have Noelle have to come rescue him.

"Hello, officer," he said, when it was his turn.

"Good evening, sir. Are you aware that you were going sixty-nine miles per hour. That's over the speed limit."

"I was in a hurry, I guess," Hunter said by way of excuse.

"Could I see your driver's license, please."

Hunter complied.

The trooper took the license and went back to his squad car to check out Hunter.

In a few minutes he was back with his ticket book open. Three minutes later Hunter was on his way with a speeding ticket to pay. The delay hadn't been that long but it was probably long enough that he would run into Jack and Grace returning or returned home from dinner. They wouldn't be staying out late the night before the big day of their daughter's wedding.

How was he going to sneak the wedding dress past them?

"You could go in the back way," Valerie suggested, reappearing in the front seat next to him.

"But what if they're still up watching television or something?"

"Then you stash the dress until they go to sleep. Once they're asleep you can sneak it up to Sophie's room."

"Good thing you're not writing the comics," Hunter said, dismissing the idea.

"Why, what's wrong with my idea? I think it's a good idea." Her red lips formed a pout.

"It stinks. You'll have to think of something better than that. First of all, the dress is too unwieldy to stash anywhere without it being noticed. And second of all, even if I could stash it—what if Sophie came home before I had a chance to get it back to her room?''

''Then you'll have to disguise it.''

''That's it!''

Hunter took the exit off the highway.

He kept his eyes open for a supermarket until he saw a National all lit up to signal it was open twenty-four hours to the public. He went in, bought a package of hefty green garbage bags and returned to the car. He slit the package open and slipped two bags over the wedding dress.

Sure enough, when he arrived at the Perrys', Noelle's parents were home already. Their car was parked in the drive. He left the wedding dress in the limo and loped up to the house to check out the lay of the land. It looked cool, he decided after a brief inspection of the entry hall and stairway. In the background he heard a shower running in Jack and Grace's bedroom.

Finally luck was with him.

He hurried back out to the limo and gathered up the garbage-bagged wedding dress. The plastic was dark green so you couldn't see what was inside the light but voluminous bundle. Easing it out of the back seat of the limo, he shoved the door closed with his foot.

The thud seemed to echo in the quiet night and he swore at his stupidity. Still, no one came to the door. He continued to have a clear path.

Getting the bundle through the front door proved no easy task, but he managed finally and breathed a sigh of relief. Starting up the stairs, he was stopped by a woman's voice.

"Oh, Hunter, it's you. I thought I heard a car door. What have you got there?" Grace asked as she came along the hall toward him.

"It's nothing, Grace. It's, ah, balloons for the reception-hall decor. Balloons, that's all."

The bundle tipped precariously.

"Here, let me help you with them—" Grace started forward.

"Oh, no. No, I'm fine—really." He got a better grip and began climbing the stairs.

Grace looked uncertain. "Well, if you're sure."

"I'm sure," he called back.

Hunter navigated the stairs and hurried down the hallway to Sophie's room where he saw the empty hanger Noelle had told him would be on the door hook. Quickly, he pulled the dress from the bags and shook it to fluff it out. Lifting it to the hanger took some doing since it was an off-the-shoulder bridal gown. He managed the feat once he found the little loops sewn inside the dress.

His mission successfully accomplished, he stood back and studied the gown. It looked pretty good to him. There were no rips or dirt stains. Sophie would never know her wedding gown had been bowling.

But he would.

A car pulled up out in front of the house and he heard Sophie and Noelle call out good-nights.

All of a sudden he was exhausted—so exhausted he almost forgot the green plastic bags he had to dash back for at the last minute.

* * *

"You'd think you were the nervous bride getting married in the morning instead of Sophie, the way you keep tossing and turning," Hunter complained from his side of the bed as Noelle plumped a pillow for what seemed like the fiftieth time.

He glanced at the digital clock on the dresser. "It's four o'clock in the morning. Don't you think it's time you got some sleep, Noelle? What are you worrying about? Sophie's wedding gown is back safe and sound. No one need ever know it hasn't been there all night."

"The wedding dress isn't worrying me any longer. I can't believe Mother almost caught you."

"Well, she didn't. So quit worrying and go to sleep. I'm exhausted and you should be, too."

She had to tell someone. She had to talk to someone. All night she'd tried to work out in her mind the best thing to do about Polly Palmer's news. There just didn't seem to be any easy answer. She was going to be wrong no matter what decision she made.

"Hunter?"

"What is it?"

"Can I trust you?"

"I told you I wasn't going to tell anyone about the wedding gown. What do I have to do to make you believe me?"

"This isn't about the wedding gown, Hunter. If you would listen to what I'm saying, you'd know that."

"Noelle, it's four in the morning. I don't know much of anything at four in the morning. If you want to tell me something, just say it. My mind is too foggy to guess what in the hell it is you're getting at."

"Oh, Hunter, I feel so stupid. I don't know what to do."

"Wait a minute, this is about *why* you were at a bowling alley in Sophie's wedding dress, isn't it?"

She nodded.

"I think I want to hear about this." Giving up on sleep for the foreseeable future, he sat straight up in bed and stacked pillows behind his back to brace himself.

Beginning was so embarrassing. She closed her eyes and plunged in. "Well, as you know, I was in Sophie's room. I'd gone to turn out the light. And I don't know why—maybe because I've never tried on a wedding dress, whatever—I gave in to the urge. I didn't think anyone would ever know. I was home all alone."

"No one will know," Hunter said, pulling her into his arms and comforting her. "It's our secret."

"Thank you," she sniffed.

He hugged her and patted her head as if she were a child that needed comforting.

"Anyway, that's when the Palmer brothers showed up."

"The Palmer brothers? Aren't they the guys on the box of cough drops?" Hunter said, trying to make her smile.

"They told me I had to come with them, that they had to show me something—that Sophie had to know something before she married Marky in the morning."

"Are you saying they *took* you—kidnapped you?"

"They insisted I come. And they wouldn't let me change out of the wedding gown. They thought they had Sophie."

"Then what happened?" Hunter asked, tension in his voice.

Noelle wiped at the tears on her cheeks. "After they got me in the car they assured me they weren't going to hurt me. They didn't. A woman got in the car then. Their sister, Polly."

"Polly and Marky, right?" Hunter said, leaping ahead of her.

"Yes. Polly's seven months pregnant, Hunter. She says the baby is Marky's."

"Is it?"

"I don't know—I don't know what to believe. I don't know what to do. What if I don't tell Sophie and it's true? What if I do tell her and it's not? What if she calls off the wedding at the last minute. There's all those hundreds of people, all that food, the presents.... Mother and Father will..."

"You'll have to tell her, Noelle. You know that, don't you? I know it's a terrible position to be put in, but Sophie has to know. Do you want me to tell her for you?"

"You'd do that?"

"Hey, I'm the guy who bagged a wedding dress. I'd do anything." He almost said, "For you." He wasn't sure why he hadn't. Maybe he was as much of a chicken as Noelle when it came to showing real emotion. Sex was easy. Romance—now that was hard.

"No, I have to be the one to do it. It has to come from me. Even if she hates me for it."

"She won't hate you," Hunter assured her, kissing her forehead. "You worry too much."

"Wouldn't you hate me, if I told you the person you were in love with was—"

"I could never hate you."

"You're just being sweet, Hunter, 'cause you feel sorry for me."

"I've always been sweet, you just haven't noticed," he assured her. "Come on, now, let's get some sleep. First thing tomorrow morning is going to come soon enough. I'll wake you at seven and you can go have a talk with Sophie before your parents are up."

"I wish I didn't know, Hunter. It was all so exciting before...."

"Come on, lie down here next to me," Hunter said, rearranging the pillows and sheet. "I'll hold you until you fall asleep."

"Jack, are you awake?"

"I am now."

"Can you believe you're going to be giving away our baby girl in the morning?"

"Not if I don't get some sleep."

"Jack?"

"What is it?"

"Do you think we have enough food? What if all those people who didn't R.S.V.P. show up?"

"There will be leftovers. There are always leftovers."

"How do you know that?"

"Because that's what I always get to eat."

"Why, Jack Perry, you take that back—"

"Make me...."

"Jack!"

"Well, you're the one who won't let me sleep."

"Jack?"

"What is it, Gracie, love?"

"It's going to be a beautiful wedding, isn't it?"

"It ought to be, it's costing enough."

"How do you know?" she asked worriedly.

"I know. Let's just say you owe me...."

Grace laughed—a satisfied laugh.

"It would never work, you know," Valerie said, kneeling beside the bed with her chin resting in her hands.

"Will you go away and let me get some sleep."

"Come on, Hunter, this is the best fantasy you've ever dreamed up. You and Miss Uptight Banker. It'll never work, I'm telling you." Valerie pushed her blond hair back from her face and gave him a defiant look.

"How do you know?" Hunter felt compelled to defend what he wanted to work. It was certainly a new feeling for him. Wanting a relationship to last longer than the fling of a few days or weeks. He didn't know what to make of it. Was it because he was getting older, or because he was growing up? "Maybe Noelle is exactly what I need," he insisted. "I need someone like Daphne to take care of me. Look after me when I'm working on a project. You know what a mess things get in then."

"Then hire an assistant," Valerie said, getting up and pacing, warming to her argument. "An assistant can organize your life for you if Daphne cuts you off. She won't, anyway. She's been threatening to for ages and she still cleans up your messes."

"I think she's serious lately. After all, I'm twenty-eight. And so is Daphne. She's going to want a family."

"So's Noelle. She's going to want a family, too. Her biological clock should start sounding louder to her pretty soon."

What if Noelle did want a family? Did he? Why hadn't he even considered it before now? He danced away from giving it too close an inspection. Denial worked well for him; why change now? "She's not going to want a family. She's not even going to want to get married. Look at her loony family. Noelle is a career person just like me. We could live together and—"

Valerie stopped pacing and gave Hunter a considering look. "She could take care of you. Sounds like such an attractive offer, Hunter. How could she refuse?"

Valerie was right. But not completely; not about how selfish he was. Okay, maybe he had been in the past, but he didn't feel that way anymore. "I'd take care of Noelle, too," he said, defending himself.

"You mean when you remembered she was there. You know how lost you get in your projects. No woman is going to put up with that. You're too self-absorbed, Hunter. You might as well face it. Like I said, it will never, ever work."

"I could change."

"Stop laughing, Valerie."

"It's not that funny," he continued. "People can change if they want to badly enough. They can."

"Come on, Hunter. You're trying to tell me you could give up what you love—give it all up for a woman? Who are you trying to kid? It's just sex."

"No, it's not! It's something more than that."

"What do you mean, 'something more'? Do you love her, Hunter?"

Did he? He sat straight up in bed.

"Hunter, you aren't answering me."

"I don't know. Maybe."

"All this may be a moot point anyway, Hunter," Valerie said, crossing her arms in front of her.

"Why?"

"I haven't heard Noelle tell you she loves you."

"Give me time, Valerie. I've only had two days with her."

"Hunter, you aren't thinking straight. You're tired and sleepy. Noelle is a banker. How would it look for her to show up with you on her arm—a cartoonist? Do you really think anyone in her business is going to take her seriously after that? The banking community is very stuffy. It's a small, closed circle. And image is everything in the banking world. She's worked hard to make it all the way to vice president. What makes you think she'd throw all that away for you?"

Hunter slumped back against the pillows. "Maybe you're right. Maybe it would never work. I guess I'm not thinking straight. I'm going to get some sleep."

"Good idea. Then I can get some, too."

But neither of them did for at least an hour, because Hunter kept wanting to wake Noelle and ask her to marry him, to find out if there was a chance she felt the same way he did. Sleep claimed him before he got up the courage to act on his impulsive urge.

Hunter Ashton was the sweetest, most wonderful man.

After Hunter had finally fallen asleep, she'd gotten up to go stand at the window, gazing out at the moonlight.

Hunter was perfect. Why had she been too stubborn to see that until now?

She didn't want the weekend to end...didn't want Hunter to go out of her life.

A bright light in the night sky caught her attention. She watched as a shooting star streaked across the inky dark.

And then she squeezed her eyes closed and made a wish.

"I wish I were marrying Hunter in the morning. I wish Hunter was in love with me."

8

Noelle sat curled up in a chair beside Sophie's bed watching her baby sister sleep. She'd watched her for the past half hour. It had been six-thirty when she'd first awoken and slipped down to Sophie's room. She wanted to talk to her before the wedding day craziness started.

She didn't really want to talk to her—she had to.

Hunter was right. She had to tell Sophie what she knew about Polly Palmer and Marky. Even if Sophie hated her for it.

While she waited for Sophie to wake up, allowing her the pleasant dreams she hoped her sister was having, Noelle glanced around Sophie's room. It was typical, she supposed, of the average teenager's room.

The wallpaper and bedspread were a pretty striped pattern she'd bet their mother had picked out. Juxtaposed with the wallpaper was a bright Beavis and Butthead poster. A stack of CDs was scattered on the floor next to a portable CD player and discarded clothing. A teddy bear rested in the window.

It wasn't the neat and tidy room Noelle had kept at Sophie's age, but then the two of them were quite different. Still, seeing her sister sleeping brought back all sorts of shared memories. She'd not known how lonely she was in Chicago. Work had kept her distracted from the fact that she actually did miss her loony family.

Missed her mother's power-shopping. Missed her father's grandiose ideas, even if he was one of the few people to ever invest in a fast-food franchise that failed. His new venture, a birdfood franchise, seemed to be holding its own. And she'd missed a lot of Sophie's teenage years.

Sophie—who, it seemed, had grander ideas than their father. A singer. A career path filled with risk and possible heartbreak. There were no guarantees for anyone who followed a creative path. But then Hunter had, and he seemed to have done all right. Besides, uncertainty and change didn't scare Sophie the way it did her.

The fog outside began to clear and sunlight filtered into the bedroom. Sophie stirred and Noelle hoped the sunlight was a sign that everything would turn out all right on her baby sister's wedding day.

When Sophie opened her eyes, Noelle said, "Good morning, sleepyhead. We need to talk."

Sophie rubbed her eyes and sat up. "I hate to tell you, but I know all about the birds and the bees and penises." She grinned, then yawned.

"This is serious, Sophie."

Sophie paled. "Has something happened to Mother or Father?"

"No. It's about Marky."

"Something's happened to Marky?" Sophie grabbed Noelle. "What is it?"

"Nothing's happened to Marky. It's not something like that. I'm sorry if I scared you. But I do have something to tell you that—"

"What is it?" Sophie dropped her hands and settled back on the bed. "You *are* going to be at the wedding. You didn't get called back to Chicago for work, did you? You wouldn't miss my wedding, Noelle?"

She had missed a lot of things for Sophie—proms, plays, Sophie cheering at football games as head cheerleader. Noelle knew, that instant, that it had mattered to Sophie. Sophie had missed her not being a part of the family and living in another city. From the age of eleven Sophie had for all intent grown up a lonely only child, Noelle saw for the first time.

And now she was going to ruin the one thing she was there for. She was going to ruin Sophie's wedding day—or at the very least, put a damper on it.

She glanced over at the wedding gown, and quickly looked away, returning her attention to Sophie.

"It's not about me, it's about Marky, remember. I have something I have to tell you that I found out only yesterday evening. I don't know any way to tell you other than to just say it straight out."

Sophie's hands were twisting in the pale pink sheet, her perfectly manicured nails, a flash of bright red matching the two spots of color in her cheeks. She stared at Noelle, waiting anxiously.

"Okay." Noelle took a deep breath. "Yesterday evening when you were at your bachelorette party, the Palmer brothers paid me a visit."

The name didn't register with Sophie.

"They said there was something you should know before you married Marky today. Sophie, their sister Polly is pregnant. The claim is that she's pregnant with Marky's baby."

Sophie didn't say anything at first.

Noelle moved to sit beside her on the bed. "Sophie, I'm so sorry. I'd give anything not to have had to tell you. But I couldn't keep it from you. I couldn't let you marry without knowing. Please don't hate me, Sophie."

"It's not true," Sophie vowed.

"What?" Noelle pulled away to look at Sophie. "Do you think I would make up a lie like that? Do you think I would want to hurt you?"

"Polly's not pregnant," Sophie insisted, her chin thrust in the air.

"She's pregnant, all right."

"How do you know?"

"Her brothers took me to her last night. They wanted to prove to you that she was pregnant. They knew you wouldn't believe it unless—" Noelle stopped. She didn't want to get into the fact that they'd thought they were showing Sophie the evidence of Polly's pregnancy.

"How pregnant?" Sophie demanded on a sniff, her eyes glassy with unshed tears.

Noelle couldn't gauge the source of emotion calling up Sophie's tears. Was it anger, fear, jealousy...? Probably all of those emotions and more.

"I don't know for sure how pregnant she is, but she looked like she was about seven months. She's tall and maybe she's further along and not showing it."

"It's not Marky's baby—she's lying." It was a statement of hope. Noelle followed Sophie's gaze to the wedding dress hanging on the door.

For Sophie's sake she prayed the hopeful accusation was true. But in her gut she didn't believe it.

"She'd do anything to stop the wedding. I believe in Marky. She just wants him to get a job, any old job. He's a really good musician. I know the band is going to be a success. I know it, Noelle."

"What if she's telling the truth, Sophie?"

"I don't know. This isn't supposed to be happening," Sophie said, pouting, not liking being a grown-up at all. "The photographer, the cake, the music, the hall, the flowers, my dress, all the food... Everything is all set. Mother and Father have spent so much money. Oh, Noelle, what am I going to do?"

Noelle hugged her. "You're going to talk to Marky. The two of you have to work it out." She glanced up at the neon-pink clock on the wall. "Whatever you do, you'd better do it soon. The wedding starts in a few hours. I'll go down and see if Mother needs any help with breakfast and you can call Marky, okay?"

Sophie wiped her tears and nodded.

"You don't hate me, do you, Sophie?"

Sophie forced a smile and shook her head no. As Noelle left the room, she heard Sophie pick up the phone.

"What's taking Sophie so long to come down?" Grace asked, as everyone sat around the breakfast table.

"She was calling Marky," Noelle answered, pulling a carton of milk from the refrigerator and filling a glass pitcher with it.

"She's going to be seeing him in a few hours."

"I know, Mother, but she needed to talk to him about something."

"Oh, what?" Grace asked, turning, concern in her eyes.

"Something about the honeymoon, I think," Noelle lied, not wanting to worry her mother until it was time to worry. This could be a tempest in a teapot. Sophie could be right; Polly could be lying. If she was, Marky and Sophie could work it out. Love could conquer anything—or so she'd heard.

Noelle set the pitcher of milk on the table beside a big box of doughnuts. Half of the doughnuts in the box were jelly, so she knew her father had gone to fetch them. He adored jelly doughnuts and had the jelly belly to prove it.

"Dad, what do you think of Marky?" Noelle asked, coming around the table to give him a peck on the cheek.

Jack looked up from the newspaper. "He's not good enough for my baby."

"All fathers say that about their daughters, Jack," Grace said, pouring milk into her cup of steaming coffee.

"Yeah, what do you really think, Father?"

"He's okay, I guess. He's eighteen, hardly even a person yet. Too young to be getting married. He doesn't even have a regular job."

"Listen to that." Grace laughed. "You weren't any different when we got married. It worked out okay, don't you think?"

"I was mature," Jack said in defense.

"Right," Grace pretended to agree, rolling her eyes at Noelle.

"I saw that," Jack said from behind the newspaper.

Noelle grinned at her mother while pouring a glass of cold milk to go with the apple-fritter doughnut she'd selected. It was heavy and rich and maybe would weigh down the butterflies in her stomach.

Just as she lifted it to take a bite, Sophie came tearing down the stairs, heading for the front door.

"Wait, where are you going?" Grace called out.

"I have to see Marky."

"But—"

It was no good, Grace was talking to dead air as Sophie sprinted out the door.

"I can't believe—"

"It's okay, Mother. I'll help you with all the details. Don't worry, I'm sure Sophie won't be gone long."

"I know, dear, but Sophie and I have a hair appointment in an hour. I hope she remembers."

"She's not going to forget something that important, Mother. Come on, Father and I will help. Let's make a list while we finish breakfast so we don't forget anything."

"Your father's list is short. He only has two things to do."

"What's that?" he asked, putting down the newspaper and reaching for another jelly doughnut.

"You've got to write checks," Grace answered.

"I've already written enough checks," he grumbled.

Grace ignored his complaint and began counting them off. "We need a check for the pastor, one for the church, another for the soloist, the organist, and one for the florist."

Hunter came walking into the kitchen in the middle of Grace's listing of who was to be paid.

When Grace was done, Jack looked up at Hunter. "That's why you should have sons—they're cheaper to marry off."

"I'll remember that, Jack," Hunter said, grinning and taking a jelly doughnut.

Jack beamed at Noelle. "He likes jelly doughnuts," he said approvingly.

"I like living dangerously," Hunter said with a wink. He took a big bite of his doughnut and the jelly oozed out. "You just never know where the jelly is going to end up."

"Yes, you do," Grace mumbled. "It ends up on the newspaper sticking together the funny pages."

For some reason that tickled Hunter.

"What was that other thing I had to do, Grace?" Jack asked, pouring another cup of coffee into his mug.

"Birdseed. Did you remember to bring home the birdseed?"

"Birdseed?" Hunter looked puzzled.

"For throwing at the bride and groom. Uncooked rice kills the birds when they peck it from the ground after the wedding."

"Good idea, birdseed," Hunter agreed.

"The birdseed is in the garage," Jack said, pleased he'd remembered.

"Good, you and Hunter can wrap up the little lace bundles for throwing."

"We can?" the two men chorused.

"You can," Grace and Noelle chorused.

"You know that might not be a bad item to carry in my store..." Jack mused, as Hunter shot Noelle a questioning look.

Noelle shrugged her shoulders to tell him she didn't know how things were going with Sophie.

"Has anyone seen Sophie?" he asked.

"I talked to her this morning and then she went off to see Marky," Noelle explained.

"Oh."

"I just hope she remembers our hair appointment," Grace muttered.

"Everything is going to be fine, Mother," Noelle assured her, though she herself was still feeling queasy.

"That was Sophie," Noelle said, hanging up the telephone in the living room. "She met Mother at the beauty salon."

"Guess that means the wedding's still on," Hunter said, trying to tie one of the thin white ribbons around a lace-covered pinch of birdseed.

"Of course, the wedding's still on," Jack responded. "Don't even think such a thing. Grace would—"

"I think we've got enough of these," Noelle said, adding her lace packet to the basket. "Why don't you and Hunter go ahead and get your showers now so there is enough hot water for everyone. I'll clean up here."

"Good idea," Jack said, happy to be done with the tedious task. Jack pushed back his chair. "I picked up your tuxedo with mine, Hunter. You might want to try it on since you ordered it on such short notice. You never know what can go wrong at a wedding."

Hunter looked over at Noelle. Both issued a silent hope that a wrong-size tuxedo was the only mishap on Sophie's wedding day.

Hunter followed Jack to get his tuxedo from the master bedroom. When he returned with it hung over one finger, Noelle had cleaned up the birdseed and scraps of lace and ribbon on the dining-room table.

"Do you think everything is okay?" he asked, tipping her chin and looking into her worried eyes. "You don't, do you?"

"Sophie hasn't talked to Marky."

"Why not?"

"She hasn't been able to find him."

Jack Perry was in his tuxedo, the very image of a proud father. He sat at the desk in the master bedroom writing out checks. "I think I could do this in my sleep."

"What, dear?" Grace asked absently, deciding against the pearl earrings she'd planned to wear with her sophisticated designer suit. Sophie had picked out the suit and nagged Grace until she'd bitten the bullet and bought it. It was beautiful, and Sophie might be the only daughter who married. This might be her only chance to be the mother of the bride. Noelle didn't seem so inclined.

"Write checks," Jack replied. "How much do I make the one for the organist for again?"

"A hundred dollars," Grace said, sorting through her earrings for the pair she'd decided on for sentimental reasons. They were the pair she'd worn on her wedding day.

"You know, Grace, when this wedding is over, you may just have to get a job," Jack teased.

Grace gave Jack a look. "No swearing on Sophie's wedding day, dear." They'd agreed when they married that Grace would never work—and she'd kept her part of the bargain.

Jack closed his checkbook and got up. He moved to zip up the inch of zipper Grace had missed at the top of her dress. He buzzed a kiss on her cheek. "How'd I get so smart at such a young age to pick you for my bride?"

"I've got a secret to share with you, Jack," Grace said, turning and putting her arms around his neck.

"I picked you."

Hunter sat stretched out on the bed. The tuxedo fit him perfectly, Noelle thought, as she came out of the shower with a towel wrapped around her. When she

turned on the blow dryer to start drying her hair,
Hunter turned up the volume on the television so he
could hear the St. Louis Cardinals' home game against
the Chicago Cubs.

"You know in this house you have to cheer for the
St. Louis Cardinals," Noelle called over to him.

Hunter glanced over at Noelle. "Hey, I'm cheering
for the towel," Hunter said, grinning lasciviously.
"Do you think if I concentrate on it hard enough, it'll
fall?"

"Not a chance," she said, laughing as she cau-
tiously raised her arms to dry the top of her head.

Hunter's attention went back to the baseball game
and Noelle dropped her false cheer. Where was
Marky? Why hadn't he been home? Why couldn't
Sophie find him on his wedding day? Was he with
Polly? She couldn't stand it if Sophie got left at the
altar. It didn't bear thinking about.

She concentrated instead on putting her hair up in
a French twist when she had it almost dry. It took all
her effort, knowing Sophie was down the hall getting
dressed in her bridal gown.

The wedding gown that knew too much.

She was beginning to think the wedding gown had
some sort of spell on it.

Now she was really getting fanciful—or was it hysterical? She wiped at the smear of lipstick her un-
steady hand had made, repairing it. The lipstick was
a matte red that matched the racy dress Hunter had
bought for her. She was working on her nerve to put
it on. It was the last thing she planned to do before she
went to the wedding.

She still had her doubts about it and the matching red satin shoes with the ribbon-wrap bows. The shoes were as bright as the ones Dorothy had worn in *The Wizard of Oz.*

She put in the diamond studs her father and mother had given her for graduation, dusted on a hint of blush and stood back to see the effect of her handiwork.

"That smells good," Hunter said, getting up from the bed and coming to where she stood in front of the mirror applying perfume.

"Thank you. Are you all ready for the wedding?"

"I'm ready. Nervous, but ready."

"Why? Because you're in the wedding?"

"Could be."

"It's not like you're the groom or anything."

"Sometimes I wonder what that would feel like."

"Really? I thought only girls daydreamed about their weddings."

"Well, it's not like I've given it much thought—until just lately."

Had he meant what she thought he meant? Noelle wondered, her heart leaping with hope.

"How about you?" he coaxed.

Afraid, she purposely misunderstood him. "I've been planning my wedding since I was a little girl."

Hunter laughed. "No wonder you couldn't resist trying on Sophie's wedding dress."

"Yes, and look at the trouble that got me into. I guess I should take it as a warning that some things just aren't meant to be," she hinted.

"You don't believe in fate? That if two people are right for each other that they will find a way to be together?"

"Do you?" she asked, looking at his reflection.

"Yes, I do," he answered, holding her gaze in the mirror.

A half smile formed on her lips.

"I think all weddings are meant to be. You make your own happiness, Noelle. And if something isn't meant to be..."

Her half smile gave away her worry.

"How can I make it all better?" he asked, kissing the nape of her neck as he stood behind her. "There's only an hour till the wedding, so there isn't time to make love," he teased, making her smile full-blown. "And besides, I'd muss your hair. We can't have everyone talking about that hussy sister who looked like she'd just gotten—ah, out of bed."

"You don't have to try to make me feel better," Noelle replied, placing her hand on his cheek in a gentle caress that said more than she'd have given away if she weren't so worried.

"But I want to," he said, sincere.

"This is something you can't kiss and make better. We'll just have to wait until we get to the church to see what will happen. Maybe everything will be all right."

"I'll make it all right," Hunter promised. Not for nothing had he created a comic-book character who made everything all right.

"I'm going down to Sophie's room to see how she's doing," Noelle said, stepping from his embrace.

"Okay, I'll go pretend to cheer for the Cardinals in case your father has the room bugged."

When she got to the doorway of Sophie's room, she saw Sophie hang up the phone with a frown.

"You still haven't talked to Marky..." Noelle said, coming into the room.

"No. Either he's not home yet, or he's getting ready and not answering the phone." Sophie tugged at the bodice of the wedding gown and went to pick up her veil.

"What are you going to do?" Noelle crossed the room to help Sophie with her veil.

"I'm going to trust Marky."

The sisters looked at each other for a long moment. "You're going through with the marriage."

"Yes."

Noelle didn't say anything. She decided she'd already said enough. It was Sophie's life. Sophie's decision. And, she sincerely thought, Sophie's mistake.

"Girls, we need to hurry," Grace said, coming into the room as Noelle settled the fingertip veil on Sophie's head. The old-fashioned veil was a beautiful complement to the wedding gown.

"Noelle—you're not even dressed. I'll help Sophie, you go get dressed. Hurry, now."

"You look so beautiful I think I'm going to cry," Noelle heard her mother say as she left the room.

"Mother, don't cry—"

Hunter was still stretched out on the bed watching the baseball game on television.

"What's the score?" she asked, rummaging through her luggage for panty hose.

"It's all tied up."

"Don't tell me that. We'll never get Father to the wedding."

"It's a tape, Noelle."

"Oh." She found the panty hose and took them and the red dress into the bathroom to get dressed. There was no graceful way to put on panty hose.

She didn't look at herself in the mirror when she had the dress on. She'd lose her nerve. Taking a calming breath, she left the bathroom to get her shoes.

"Could you help me with these?" She stood before the bed, dangling the red shoes by their inch-wide ribbon ties. Hunter looked away from the game on television and up at her. The pupils of his blue eyes widened, softened.

He patted the bed beside him.

She sat down and handed him the shoes.

He pulled her foot onto his lap and slipped her foot into the red satin shoe. Then, after wrapping the red ribbon ties in an X across her foot, he circled her narrow ankle and tied a bow.

He repeated the process with the other shoe.

When he was done, she gazed up at him.

Between them was the memory of the dressing room at Concepts.

He lowered his head and kissed the inside of her ankle. "You sure we have to go to this wedding?" he asked. The glint in his eye coaxed her to play. To be impulsive.

Oh, and how she wanted to play.

But her parents would never forgive her if she missed the wedding.

Sophie needed her.

Sometimes you just had to be responsible.

"We could be late," Hunter said, kissing the inside of her knee.

"I can't—" She slid from Hunter's grasp.

"I know."

"Hunter?"

He looked over to where she stood at the window.

"Thank you."

"For what?"

"For this weekend. I don't know what I would have done without you here."

He got up and went to her, put his arms around her. "You would have done just fine, Noellie."

She sniffed.

"Don't cry, you'll ruin your makeup. It'll be wet and rub off on my tuxedo and people will point and say that hussy sister has been necking with that stranger from the big city."

Noelle smiled. "St. Louis *is* a big city, Hunter."

"You just go on believing that."

She punched his arm.

"Feel better?"

She nodded.

"Okay, then let's go. We don't want to be late. Well, *I* want to be late, but you being such a responsible person and all . . ."

He offered his arm and she took it.

The way she'd been taking the shoulder he'd offered all weekend.

When they got downstairs the rental limo was there for Jack, Grace and Sophie. Jack and Grace beamed with pride as they settled Sophie in the limo.

Hunter and Noelle waved them off and followed in the white limo.

The church was small. Their regular church had been unable to accommodate them because it was all booked up with spring weddings.

But the small church had a lot of charm and the minister was friendly, if a bit absentminded.

Only family and close friends had been invited to the wedding ceremony. The big shindig would be the reception that evening.

Hunter followed the black limo in front of them to the church and parked right behind it.

On the curb in front of the church waiting in his tuxedo was Marky.

Noelle didn't know whether to be happy or sad that Sophie wasn't going to be left standing at the altar.

9

The service was late getting started.

The guests were restless, murmuring among themselves and glancing back past the pews behind them to the lobby of the church expectantly.

A baby cried.

Someone coughed.

The groomsmen told awful wedding-night jokes among themselves. The groom was still absent from the altar group.

The heavy church door thudded as a late arrival came hurrying in and took a seat at the rear.

The murmuring grew louder as minutes ticked by and the organist didn't begin playing.

Everyone looked at each other curiously as an usher came up and escorted Hunter to the back of the church.

A hush settled over the crowd—a hush of worried anticipation.

It didn't look good, Hunter thought when he reached the lobby at the rear where everyone was gathered. The bridesmaids—six wide-eyed nervous girls in party dresses—stood off to one side. They were looking at the scene that greeted Hunter.

Sophie was in tears in her father's arms.

Jack was trying to console her.

Another young woman was clinging to the intended groom. A pregnant young woman. Polly.

Noelle was trying to calm her mother, while Grace looked completely flustered, unable to muster a solution to "all that potato salad."

"What's going on?" Hunter asked the question that had a pretty obvious answer: nothing was going on, most especially a wedding.

"I'm not getting married—" Sophie sobbed. "Marky's... He's... not marrying me. He belongs with the mother of his baby."

"Hunter, could you stay with Mother while I go up to the front of the church to announce the wedding has been called off?" Noelle pleaded.

"No."

"Well, then, could you announce it?"

"No."

"Hunter, I don't know what else to do."

"I do. Notice how easily 'I do' tripped off my lips, Noelle. Suddenly I'm not nervous at all."

"What are you talking about...?"

"I think fate has just come knocking, Noelle. What do you think?"

"You mean?"

"Why don't you trade dresses with Sophie?" Winking, he couldn't resist adding, "I think the dress will fit you."

"But—"

"Yes, it'll fit," Grace encouraged as Marky and Polly slipped out of the church. Grace clapped her hands together with excited relief. "We can have a wedding, after all."

"But—"

"Listen to your mother, Noelle," Jack said, still comforting Sophie. "Everything is in place. It would be a shame—"

"But—"

"Don't you love me, Noelle?" Hunter asked bravely.

All eyes were on her and Hunter was looking very vulnerable.

"I'll meet you at the altar," she agreed, and everyone smiled as the mood in the church lobby elevated.

Hunter hurried to rejoin the groomsmen waiting anxiously at the front of the church.

The organist began playing and the guests turned their attention to the back of the church once again with a collective sigh of relief.

The bridesmaids in their floaty pale pink dresses started down the center aisle that had been laid with a white runner. Pastel ribbons fluttered from their spring bouquets as they walked. The entire church was decorated with an assortment of fresh white flowers whose fragrance filled the air.

The guests smiled at the bridesmaids as they passed by the pews. One girl made a misstep and nearly fell, but then bridesmaids were always nervous. The girl giggled in embarrassment, then regained her composure. Finally all the bridesmaids had taken their places at the altar and it was time for the bride.

The organ was silent for a few minutes and people were starting to crane their necks to see what the holdup was at the back of the church. Just as a buzz of questioning started, the organist began again.

"Dum ... dum ... de ... dum ...   Dum ... dum ... de ... dum ..."

Jack Perry appeared with a flash of white tulle at his side and everyone relaxed. A few older women smiled in approval at the old-fashioned veil that covered the bride's face—even if the wedding gown was off-the-shoulder.

The pair began their slow walk down the center aisle, the bride clinging to her father's arm.

"Oh..."

"Oh, my..."

"Did you see ... ?"

"Look at that ... !"

"Why do you suppose ... ?"

"It's scandalous, that's what it is...."

"Mommy, look at her shoes—aren't they pretty ... ?"

"Well, I never. I can't believe Grace would let her daughter wear such a thing...."

"I think they're cool. You should be able to wear whatever you want to your wedding. I'm wearing combat boots to mine...."

"Can I wear red shoes like those when I get married, Mommy?"

The bride was glad of the tulle veil that hid her face. She could feel it flushing with color at all the whispered comments she heard as she walked down the aisle, her red shoes plainly visible.

The comments continued as she made her way on her father's arm to the front of the church. Her father squeezed her hand in a show of support. The look on her mother's face as they passed her pew at the front of the church was one of complete astonishment.

A gasp went up from the guests when Hunter stepped forward to take the bride from her father—in their fascination with the bride's red shoes, no one had noticed the groom hadn't arrived.

What was going on?

"Hunter, what are you doing!" Valerie Valor asked, incredulous, tugging on his arm.

There was whispered concern sweeping the crowd as Jack Perry took his seat in the pew next to Grace and bent his head to speak with her.

"Hunter—" Valerie repeated urgently.

The minister cleared his throat to gain the guests' full attention before starting the service. His face had a sheen of perspiration and his gray hair was in slight disarray from the minor fender bender he'd been in on his way to the church—he wasn't seeing as well as he used to.

Still somewhat flustered, he leafed through his Bible nervously. Unable to find his notes, the minister glanced down at the floor around him—to no avail.

He looked at the couple in front of him and smiled reassuringly. Finally giving up on his notes, he cleared his throat a second time and began.

"Friends and family, we are all gathered today to join...ah...this lovely couple...in holy matrimony...."

"Hunter...don't tune me out, this is serious," Valerie said.

The minister pulled at his ear and then announced, "The happy couple will now recite the vows they've composed themselves.... Ahem..."

Hunter, who'd been looking at the veiled bride, spun his head to look at the minister.

The minister nodded, encouraging him to begin.

"Now what are you going to do, Hunter? How are you going to write yourself out of this one?" Valerie asked.

Hunter turned back to the bride and took her hand. It was shaking, but then so was his. He gave her hand a slight, reassuring squeeze, looked down at her red shoes and then back up at her and smiled.

"From the first time I heard your voice, I knew I would be yours. I knew it was good that we—I knew we were meant to share an adventure—life's adventure. I'm so happy that you chose me as the man for you. I promise to honor your choice and to be here for you, to be the man you need."

"I guess that's the best in the way of romance one could hope for," Valerie said grudgingly, "from a cartoonist."

"You took my breath away from the first time I saw you," the bride countered. "At the time I had a wedding on my mind and you said you loved weddings. I didn't know how much, but I'm glad I found such a romantic superhero."

The minister looked even more puzzled and the guests began to whisper again as the minister asked for the rings.

"Rings?" Valerie repeated. "Did I nod off? I don't recall you buying any rings." Valerie threw her arms in the air, giving up.

The groomsman who'd slipped over to best man came forward and bent his head toward Hunter, who whispered something. The groomsman nodded, handed Hunter the rings from his pocket and returned to his place.

"Oh, that's pathetic, Hunter— You're not really going to exchange..."

Hunter handed the minister the rings.

The minister looked down at the rings he'd dropped with a thud in his open Bible, and then back up at Hunter.

Hunter nodded for the minister to continue.

"You are," Valerie confirmed.

The minister held up the clunky college ring with the red-faceted stone. He handed it to Hunter. "Place the ring on her finger and repeat after me—'With this ring I thee wed.'"

Hunter took the bride's left hand and looked at her as he slipped the ring on her third finger where it wobbled as he repeated, "With this ring I thee wed."

"Is this a Kodak moment or what, Hunter? I bet the DeBeers diamond company is hiring a hit on you right this minute. You've single-handedly set fine jewelry back a century," Valerie said.

"And now the bride." The minister handed her the other college ring with a blue-faceted stone. "Repeat after me, 'With this ring I thee wed.'"

The bride shoved the ring on Hunter's finger as a tear slid down her cheek.

"A perfect fit. *Quel surprise,* eh, Hunter? Guess this was just meant to be," Valerie added.

The bride and groom turned to the minister expectantly.

"Oh. You, ah, I now pronounce you man and wife—I mean, husband and wife," the minister said, flustered. "And you may now kiss your bride."

"Hunter, do you know what you've done?" Valerie demanded. "This isn't a fantasy. You can't use your eraser to make it right."

Hunter lifted the bride's veil and a wave of shock rolled over the assemblage.

"It's not only not the same groom, it's not the same bride," a shocked woman behind Grace said.

The woman leaned forward and tapped Grace. "I thought your daughter was getting married."

"My daughter did get married," Grace informed the woman. "My older daughter."

Hunter had pulled Noelle into his arms. Her earlier tears from nerves had vanished. The kiss he bestowed on her went on . . . and on . . . and on . . . ."

"Hunter this is a PG crowd," Valerie chastised.

The kiss was interrupted by the organ music, festive and loud.

"Da . . . da . . . di . . . da . . . da . . . da . . . da . . ."

Hunter wrapped Noelle's hand around his arm as they turned to face the crowd. He looked down at his college ring on her finger. "I'll get you some tape so it'll stay on," he promised.

"At least it matches my shoes," Noelle said, smiling at the red stone. Just before they returned down the aisle arm in arm, she clicked the heels of her red shoes together and said, "Hunter, I don't think we're in Kansas anymore."

While the guests remained seated, still in shock, Hunter hurried Noelle to the rear of the church.

"Now you've really gone and done it, Hunter. You've made a promise you're going to have to keep," Valerie declared, approving.

Before them, as if in slow motion, Noelle saw a glimpse of red. Sophie had stayed to watch the ceremony, even when it was supposed to have been her day. Even when Marky had told her Polly's baby was his.

How could Noelle be happy when she knew what Sophie had gone through minutes before Hunter had decided to make the substitution that would bail Sophie out.

On impulse, Noelle tossed the bridal bouquet at Sophie.

It sailed high into the air and traveled slowly to the pew where Sophie sat . . . and landed in the lap of the U.S. Navy pilot in white dress uniform sitting beside her.

The surprised pilot lifted the bouquet and turned to Sophie. His dark eyes looked into her blue ones. Seeming to suddenly remember he had the bridal bouquet, he handed it to Sophie, saying, "I believe this was meant for you."

Meanwhile Hunter grabbed a bunch of white flowers tied with satin ribbon to the last pew and handed them to Noelle as he hustled them to the waiting limo for a chance to continue that interrupted kiss.

PG just wasn't his style.

Sophie and the navy man stood with the others outside the church tossing birdseed at the limo as it drove off.

Wishing hard, she flung her tiny bundle of birdseed, and cried out, "Be happy!"

10

Hunter escorted Noelle from the registration desk at one of St. Louis's ritziest hotels toward the elevator. They were on their way to the bridal suite Hunter had just wangled for a few hours.

"Think you're pretty hot stuff, don't you?" Noelle said.

The elevator doors closed on Hunter's wicked grin. "Well, I did perform a rescue today. That's something, don't you think?"

"A rescue, huh?"

"Yeah." Hunter put his finger on her nose. "I saved your mother's potato salad."

Noelle took his finger and kissed the tip of it.

"I don't play by the rules, as you may have noticed, my bride—witness the lack of a marriage license."

"Wait till my father thinks of that!"

"Don't worry. The main thing is we saved the potato salad when Sophie decided to call off the wedding."

"Poor Sophie."

"I don't know, she didn't look very unhappy at the reception in that red dress of yours, dancing with that guy in the white dress uniform."

"No, she didn't, did she? Makes me think that Polly was right. Sophie was marrying Marky to sing in his band."

"Sophie's going to be just fine. Your parents are going to be just fine about this eventually. And in a minute you and I are going to be just fine." Hunter scooped her up in a billow of white tulle just as the elevator doors swished open on the floor of the bridal suite.

Hunter kissed Noelle soundly as he kicked the door to the suite shut behind them. "I'll give you one thing, my beautiful bride. You give great adventure," he said, as he set her down. He smiled, glancing at her feet. "And you don't give bad shoe, either...."

"I think you're having way too much fun," Noelle retorted, sliding him a saucy look.

He stepped toward her, pulled her into an embrace and slipped his hand into the strapless crumb-catcher bodice of her wedding dress. "Bride, I have only just begun to have fun."

There was a knock at the door. A discreet knock.

They looked at each other, puzzled. With a great show of reluctance Hunter withdrew his hand from the "toy chest" and went to the door.

"Yes?" he said through the closed door.

"Room service, sir."

"But I didn't order anything—"

"Compliments, sir..."

Hunter looked at Noelle, shrugged, and opened the door.

The bellman handed Hunter a silver bucket with a bottle of iced champagne nestled in it. "Compliments of the hotel."

Hunter laughed. "Thanks." He took some money from his wallet and passed it to the bellman who nodded his thanks and pulled the door closed.

Hunter leaned back against the door. "Finally we're alone. Your sister isn't at the end of the hall, your parents aren't downstairs, the saleslady isn't hovering.... We're—"

"I'm hungry. Let's call room service."

"What?"

"How do you like marriage so far, Hunter?" Valerie taunted.

"I'm hungry," Noelle repeated.

"Didn't you eat at the reception?" Hunter asked, incredulous. "How can you be hungry?"

"I couldn't eat with all those people watching me."

Hunter crossed the room, set down the bucket of champagne and picked up the phone. He ordered up the chef's specialty with instructions to leave it outside the door.

"Happy?"

"Very."

"Let's have a toast to your happiness." Hunter opened the champagne with a pop.

"I *am* happy, Hunter," Noelle said, sighing with contentment. A girl would have to be a fool not to know that it didn't get any better than the bridal suite at the Ritz with Hunter Ashton.

"So you're admitting you're not really angry with me. That I make you happy. Happy enough to let me drink champagne from your slipper?" he asked, eyebrows wagging lasciviously. He paused after filling his champagne glass, waiting before filling hers.

"Hunter Ashton you are not going to drink champagne from Noelle's shoe—for one thing, they won't hold champagne," Valerie admonished.

"Maybe I should rephrase that—I meant to say lick champagne from your shoe," Hunter said to Noelle, considering Valerie's point.

"I don't think that's a good idea, Hunter."

"Besides she'd squish when she went back to the reception," Valerie said.

That would assume, Hunter thought, someone planned on going back to the reception.

He poured her a glass of champagne, unable to do battle and win with two women.

"To happy ever after," Hunter toasted, clinking his champagne glass with hers. "And to my removing the white lace garter from your thigh...I can assure you of that."

"Plan to keep it as a souvenir of battle, do you?"

"Battle?"

"There's no marriage license," she reminded him.

"And if there was?" he said, tossing her on the high, cushy bed.

The game was suddenly over.

They weren't playing anymore.

The groom knew it.

The bride knew it.

"Hunter—"

"Yes, or no...?"

"You're a romantic—"

"Fool, I know."

For a superhero, he looked really vulnerable.

"Well . . . ?" he prompted.

"Are you sure— How much champagne did you drink at the reception, Hunter?"

"Not *that* much."

"It's this dress—"

"What?"

"It wants me to be its bride. There must be some sort of curse on it. I put it on during a weak moment— That's what happens when you give in to impulse. Everything gets so crazy and . . ."

"Wonderful," he supplied.

"Noelle?"

"What?"

"It's not the dress."

"It's not?"

"It's the shoes."

"Then I'm taking them off."

His grin was decidedly wicked. "You'll get no argument from me."

"Hunter?"

"What?"

She crooked her finger for him to come closer and he complied. She reached up and loosened his tuxedo tie. "That was a yes, Hunter. Pay attention."

"Really?"

"As real as it gets, Hunter."

"Then let the honeymoon begin." He pulled her into an embrace for the tenderest kiss a wild man could give.

"Uh-uh, Hunter." She slipped out from under him. "I didn't really know it when I was getting married. I want to *really* know it when I'm having my honeymoon. We get the wedding license first thing Monday and then we *plan* the honeymoon. The license will make our wedding today legal."

Hunter stared at her from the bed. "Are you telling me yes *and* no?"

"Ah... You're starting to pay attention." She crooked her finger for him to come closer and he did. She reached up and retied his bow tie.

"You're serious. You really want to wait."

"Sandy beaches, moonlight, skinny-dipping."

"All right, we'll wait. Two weeks, max."

"Perfect."

Epilogue

——➤ ◄——

"**Y**ou know you aren't getting any work done," Valerie complained, picking up a dirty sock and making a face.

"I'm on vacation. Give me a break, I just got married two weeks ago and I haven't even been on my honeymoon yet. We did everything backwards from the splashy family wedding on Saturday night to the wedding licence on Monday."

"I know. That's why you've been so cranky."

"I'm *not* cranky."

"Right."

"Daphne is cranky."

"Boy, is she ever. You're in deep doo-doo for not inviting her to your wedding."

"I can't help it. I didn't know I was going to get married."

"Well, you'd better introduce her to your wife soon before Daphne writes you out of the family. It's not like you have a lot of family to lose."

"I've already thought of that. Daphne is driving us to the airport today so we can fly off on our honeymoon."

"Clever boy, you've thought of everything, haven't you—except the new outfit you promised me."

"Oh, I've thought of that, too. I just haven't told you about it yet."

"So, tell me before I get too old to wear it!"

"Now who's cranky?"

"Hunter—"

"Okay, okay. What would you think of a pair of faded jeans and a tank top?"

"Jeans and a tank top? Where'd you ever come up with that?"

Hunter didn't answer. He smiled, recalling how sexy Noelle had looked silhouetted in the lighted doorway of the Venice Café wearing the jeans and tank top he'd lifted from the laundromat.

"I like it, Hunter. Good work. Maybe some kind of insignia for the tank top—think about it. Oh, and combat boots would go good with it. Yeah, that'd be perfect. You've got it, Hunter."

"No combat boots."

"Hunter, I'm not wearing those red shoes."

"I know."

"I'm certainly not wearing bowling shoes."

"I know."

"What, then?"

"Nothing. Well, maybe a little grape toenail polish would be a nice touch."

"Barefoot? Forget it, Hunter. The next step pregnant. Superheroines do *not* get pregnant."

"No, no. I was thinking of teaching you a litt martial arts—"

The doorbell rang, interrupting his mental dialogue with Valerie.

He turned down the air conditioner on his way to
answer the door.

"Daphne, you're early."

"I knew I'd have to help you pack."

"Shows what you know," he informed her, slouch-
ing down in his chair in front of his drawing board,
and scratching his chest. "I'm already packed. In case
you didn't know it, Daphne, you don't need much
gear for a honeymoon."

Daphne let his remark ride and came over to see
what he'd been working on, accidentally knocking a
pen off the drawing table and smearing India ink on
the floor.

"I'll get it," Hunter volunteered, going to the
kitchen to get a cloth to wipe up the ink. "Take a look
at Valerie's new outfit and tell me what you think."

Daphne looked up from the piece of bristol board
on the drawing table when Hunter returned to wipe up
the ink.

"Well, at least she won't catch her death of cold in
the wintertime," Daphne sniffed. "Why is it so cold
in here?"

"It's hot in here."

"It is not." Daphne flipped her blond hair back and
peered at Hunter. "Are you all right? Your eyes look
a little glassy. Maybe you should let me take your
temperature."

"Get away from me with that nurse stuff, Daphne.
I'm perfectly fine." He scratched his arm. "I'm just

excited to be going on my honeymoon. That's bound to raise any guy's temperature, don't you think?''

''I suppose. Why don't you let me take your temperature anyway.''

''Back off,'' Hunter said, holding up two fingers in a sign of the vampire cross. ''There's as much chance of me letting you do nurse things to me as there is of me finding a rare issue of the first comic to feature Superman.''

''All right, all right, be stubborn, but you look kinda peaked to me.''

''You're just mad because I packed all by myself. You nag me to grow up and then you get annoyed when I do.''

''Did you remember to pack—''

''Yes. I packed my Speedo, my suntan lotion, mega vitamins to keep up my strength—'' he winked ''—and condoms just to be safe,'' he ribbed.

''Hunter, really.''

''Come on over and look at this brochure for where we're going. Doesn't it look great? A little sun and rum, and I'll be fine.''

''I thought you said you felt all right.''

''I do. I do. Will you quit with the nurse stuff.''

''All right. Then tell me what my new sister-in-law is like.''

Hunter smiled. ''You're gonna love her.''

''What makes you so sure?''

''Because she's just like you. She's practical, smart and won't cut me any slack.''

''I'm surprised you had the sense to marry her. She sounds too good to be true.''

"You know you ought to have another one of those bachelor auctions. Maybe you could find a nice doctor—"

"There are no nice doctors. They all think they're—"

"It's Noelle," Hunter said, getting up to answer the doorbell. "Wait right here, you're going to love her," he promised, rubbing his eyes.

Hunter made the introductions and watched the two women he loved size each other up.

"Do you think Hunter looks peaked?" Daphne asked Noelle, deciding Noelle was indeed okay.

"Daphne, you think everyone looks peaked. Tell her to clock off duty as Nurse Daphne, Noelle," Hunter said, scratching his neck.

"What are you scratching?" Noelle approached Hunter for a closer inspection.

She began unbuttoning his shirt.

"Noelle, wait till we at least get to the islands to start celebrating our honeymoon!" He grinned over at Daphne and winked. "It's hell being so sexy my woman can't keep her hands off me. But what's a stud like me to do? I'm doomed to be her plaything."

Noelle felt Hunter's forehead with the back of her wrist and shook her head. "Daphne, I think you'd better get the thermometer. I was afraid of this as soon as I found out about Barbara Ann."

"Barbara Ann? There haven't been any other women, Noelle. I promise."

"I know. Barbara Ann is the little girl who lives in my apartment building."

Hunter looked completely puzzled as Daphne went to his bathroom to retrieve the thermometer from his medicine cabinet—a little too eagerly, he thought.

"How do you feel? Do you feel hot?" Noelle asked.

"Maybe a little," he admitted. "But it's nothing. I'm telling you—"

Daphne returned with the thermometer in hand. She shook it down to 98.6. "Okay, Hunter, open wide and then try to keep your mouth shut for a few minutes."

"You are going to have your hands full with him, you know, Noelle," Daphne warned. "He won't pick up after himself. He isn't house-trained at all. There probably isn't any male in the city of Chicago more spoiled rotten, and I'm afraid I'm responsible."

"Wait a minute, you can't talk about me like—"

"Mouth shut, Hunter," Daphne instructed.

He frowned at her, but followed her instructions, knowing Daphne now had an ally in Noelle. His life was going to be—

"He does have some good qualities," Noelle said, defending her husband.

Hunter smiled and nearly flipped out the thermometer.

Daphne caught it before it dropped to the floor. "Just as I thought, you have a temperature. You're not going anywhere but to bed."

"That's what honeymoons are, Daphne. You should try it sometime."

"No honeymoon trip, Hunter. You're going to bed now. You're sick," Daphne insisted.

"Sick? I can't be sick. I've waited two long weeks for... for... Noelle has been working overtime since we got married so we could take a honeymoon. I haven't hardly even seen her since we got married. I'm going—"

"She's right. You are sick," Noelle agreed.

"I would know if I was sick," Hunter argued. "So, okay, maybe I'm feeling a little hot and itchy, but—"

"Look at your chest." Noelle pointed.

Hunter looked down.

"You could play connect-the-dots," Daphne said.

"It's nothing. It's just some sort of rash or something." Hunter dismissed the red dots, rationalizing.

"It's some sort of rash, all right," Noelle agreed. "It's probably shingles."

"Shingles!"

Noelle turned to Daphne. "Barbara Ann, the little girl in my apartment building, came down with chicken pox just as I was leaving to go to St. Louis with Hunter for my sister's wedding."

"But that was two weeks ago," Hunter reasoned.

"Two weeks is the incubation period," Daphne informed him. "Noelle's right. Shingles is the adult version of chicken pox."

"Does this mean I can't—"

"That's right." Daphne read him off the recipe for recovery. It didn't involve sun, sandy beaches or rum on an island.

After she told Noelle what to do for Hunter, she left, as she hadn't had chicken pox as a child, either.

A half hour later Hunter was propped up in bed in a dark room wearing his Speedo with Noelle sitting beside him.

"How come *you* didn't get the shingles? You're the one who was exposed to Barbara Ann."

"Because I've already had the chicken pox, that's why."

"Read to me from the travel brochure," Hunter said, looking pitiful.

Noelle picked up the brochure and obliged. "'Rumbling surf, sailboats silhouetted against the sky, thatch-roofed bar, tables in the sand, wicked rum punch, snoozing in hammocks, turtles racing on the beach, swaying palm trees, thong bikinis...'"

"Come here," Hunter said, taking the travel brochure from her hand and pulling her toward him.

"I thought you were sick."

"Not that sick. Daphne didn't say anything about not having a honeymoon, she just said I had to stay at home and go to bed."

"I don't know, Hunter—"

"Just be gentle with me. You'll have to do most of the work because I'm sick, you know...."

Noelle chuckled. "Daphne was right. You are spoiled rotten."

Hunter moved his hand beneath her crop top.

"And fresh at the same time..."

"Noelle—"

"Um...what?"

"Put your bikini on and get the suntan oil while you're at it."

"Hunter Ashton, you're making me blush."

"Not yet, Noellie, but I will...."

* * *

"It's not funny." Valerie stomped her foot.

"I'm laughing."

"It's not funny, Hunter."

"I'm the cartoonist, I'll be the judge of what's funny."

Valerie glared at him. "I knew this would happen. I just knew it."

"Well, you're the one who wanted to have an adventure with Eric the Great. I told you that I didn't like the idea."

"Then you shouldn't have listened to me. You're the one who's got the pen. You're the one who's supposed to be in control."

"Right. Like I'm in control where any woman is concerned. Daphne and Noelle already plot against me all the time. And you, well, we both know I've never been able to control you."

"That's because you're not disciplined."

"If I were disciplined, I wouldn't be creative. And if I weren't creative, you wouldn't exist."

"Don't go getting all reasonable on me, Hunter. I'm not used to it. I think Noelle is beginning to—"

"If you want to blame someone, blame Noelle. She's the one who got carried away with the suntan lotion."

"I don't want to hear about it."

"I didn't want to hear about all the details with Eric the Great, either, Valerie, but I did. Face it, Valerie, you and I are like Daphne and me. We share a mind. Just like I always know what my twin is thinking, we always know what each other is thinking. We share everything. I want you to be happy, too."

"I knew this was going to happen when you wouldn't let me wear the combat boots. I knew it. As soon as I started going barefoot, I saw what it was going to lead to. I warned you, but no—"

"You're a wuss of a superheroine, Valerie. You don't see Noelle complaining. She goes to work, so you have to go to work, too."

"Noelle doesn't have to pummel people right after tossing her cookies every morning from morning sickness. All your wife has to do is go to her bank and do math."

Hunter chuckled. "Come on, Valerie. We both know math is hard. You've seen my checkbook."

"Funny, Hunter. You're a laugh riot."

"I know. That's why I make big bucks."

"I think it's time you started spending some of those big bucks on a new outfit for me. These jeans are beginning to get a little snug around the waist," Valerie said, tugging.

"Okay, if you promise to stop complaining, I'll give you a new outfit."

What kind of outfit?

"I don't know. I'll talk to Noelle about it tonight." He talked to Noelle about everything. It was wonderful, he was finding, sharing things with someone you loved. Waking up with them beside you.

"Does Noelle know what you've done?"

Hunter chuckled. "I think the morning sickness is a pretty good clue."

"I'm talking about the house," Valerie said, shooting him a pained look.

"No. She doesn't know. I want to surprise her."

"What are you waiting for?"

"The decorator."

"Noelle's not going to like that. She'll want to decorate the house herself. Gosh, don't you men know anything?"

"Eric's going to take exception to talk like that, Valerie. I'm only decorating one room as a surprise for Noelle when I bring her home from the hospital."

"You mean the nursery." Valerie smiled at the goosey look that word brought to his face.

He couldn't believe he was going to be a father. He couldn't believe anyone could be as happy as he was. It was the reason he'd gotten Valerie hitched. He thought the whole world should be as happy as he was.

"But she only just found out she was pregnant. You've got seven months yet to go before the baby is due. More if the baby is late."

Seven months of pampering Noelle. He was going to love it.

Daphne was amazed he'd even learned to pick up his own socks. Hell, *he* was amazed.

"I'm going to need all the time I can get," he assured Valerie. First I'm going to have to figure out what you do with a pregnant superheroine, and second, I'm going to need time to make up my mind whether to paint the nursery pink or blue."

"You might want to paint it half-and-half," Valerie offered with a grin.

"Why would I want to do that?"

"Think about it, Hunter. You...Daphne... There's a really good chance the baby could be twins."

"That's not funny, Valerie."

*   *   *   *   *

SPECIAL EDITION

Stories of love and life, these powerful
novels are tales that you can identify with—
romances with "something special" added in!

Fall in love with the stories of authors such
as **Nora Roberts, Diana Palmer, Ginna Gray**
and many more of your special favorites—as
well as wonderful new voices!

Special Edition brings you
entertainment for the heart!

SSE-GEN

SILHOUETTE® Desire®

Do you want...

Dangerously handsome heroes

Evocative, everlasting love stories

Sizzling and tantalizing sensuality

Incredibly sexy miniseries like **MAN OF THE MONTH**

Red-hot romance

Enticing entertainment that can't be beat!

You'll find all of this, and much *more* each and every month in **SILHOUETTE DESIRE**. Don't miss these unforgettable love stories by some of romance's hottest authors. Silhouette Desire—where your fantasies will always come true....

♥ Silhouette ROMANCE™

What's a single dad to do when he needs a wife by next Thursday?

Who's a confirmed bachelor to call when he finds a baby on his doorstep?

How does a plain Jane in love with her gorgeous boss get him to notice her?

From classic love stories to romantic comedies to emotional heart tuggers, **Silhouette Romance** offers six irresistible novels every month by some of your favorite authors!
Such as...beloved bestsellers **Diana Palmer,**
Annette Broadrick, Suzanne Carey, Elizabeth August
and **Marie Ferrarella,** to name just a few—and some sure to become favorites!

Fabulous Fathers...Bundles of Joy...Miniseries...
Months of blushing brides and convenient weddings...
Holiday celebrations... You'll find all this and much more in
Silhouette Romance—always emotional, always enjoyable,
always about love!

SR-GEN